RESIST
FASCISM

Crossed
Genres
Publications

FRAMINGHAM, MA

RESIST FASCISM

Published by Crossed Genres Publications
http://crossedgenres.com

FIRST EDITION: November 2018

ISBN-13: 978-0-9913921-4-8
ISBN-10: 0-9913921-4-0

Edited by Bart R. Leib and Kay T. Holt
Associate Editor: Crystal Huff

Cover art: "Matchstick" copyright © 2018 by Geneva Bowers
http://http://genevab.com/

Cover and interior layout by Bart R. Leib

TABLE OF CONTENTS

TO RAIN UPON ONE CITY
RIVQA RAFAEL

"Need the cred card, Em," Limor says.

Em doesn't move. Limor's mother is curled on her pallet, facing the wall. Em clutches tightly to a worn polyfibre blanket that would do little to keep her bony body warm.

"Really, Em, 'sno food left." Limor waits another thirty seconds before yelling. "EM!"

Outside, someone bangs on the pitted metal wall of their shelter, protesting Limor's disruption. It's loud enough to shake Em awake. She mumbles something incoherent and waves a thin, track-marked arm. Limor snatches the prepaid card from Em's now-revealed pocket and tucks it deep within her own clothes. It had been a mistake to let Em 'borrow' it. Em might've had enough sense to not let her friends keep it – barely – but that hadn't stopped her from treating them to post-hit snacks that would put Limor's budget out for weeks.

Gritting her teeth, Limor wraps a threadbare scarf around her body, pulling it as tight as it can go, and pulls the door open. Down here in Sub-T, between the foundations that keep the station anchored to Mikve's surface, the moon's ceaseless rain is barely perceptible, even to Limor's sharp ears. It's mostly masked by the hum of the station: the climate control, which was never designed for the twisty corridors of Sub-T; the moisture crawlers, working their way up and down the outer walls to check for leaks; the clang of boots and vehicles against metal.

Em hates hearing the rain. She says it's a reminder that she's stuck down here forever, imprisoned by uncaring authorities Up-station and planet-side. But Limor likes to listen for it. Em could be wrong, for one. Things could change. Sometimes Limor daydreams about changing them, being a hero. And so what if Em doesn't believe – in *any* god, she always says, not just our ancestors'? The idea of being surrounded by water is so alien, so mysterious, Limor can hardly imagine it. Who's to say *holy* isn't the right word for that?

Today, as Limor makes her way to the charity grocer, the A/C is blaring and she can't hear anything, even when she's on higher ground,

1

taking a shortcut scrambling across makeshift buildings, light and sure of foot.

She touches the cred card to the scanner at the Gemaḥ's doorway. As always, the volunteer cashier doesn't blink, even though as a minor Limor isn't supposed to have the card. People know about her Em. And the type of person to volunteer down here with the refugees isn't going to be a stickler for regulations, anyway.

Fifty creds left for next cycle; Limor immediately starts calculating, brow furrowed tightly. She can afford almost enough nutrient bars, and if she's lucky there might be veggies on special to provide some variety. The volunteer watches as Limor stares longingly at the baby spinach. After Em's latest antics, it's much too expensive. Instead, she reaches for a curly sweet potato, then draws her hand back, scowling. Their water purifier needs a new filter. The irony of being surrounded by fresh, clean water and having to drink other people's piss isn't lost on her. To most Up-stationers, Limor and her neighbours are a nuisance at best, a drain on the station but at least a temporary one, their presence only accepted on condition they don't reproduce. Even the Gemaḥ, that small group trying to keep the refugees fed and clothed, is barely tolerated.

"An X-50," she points behind the counter to the replacement filter that fits their machine. They're all refurbs, of course, locked behind plexiglass with the jars of mayim ḥayim. The living water is free, collected from Mikve's plentiful rivers by religious-minded volunteers, but it's rationed so people use it for its intended sacred purposes. It's understandable, but Limor resents it anyway. One time, when she was young and curious, Limor managed to convince a new vollie that she needed some. She'd never tasted sweeter water. It was the one and only time a savta had yelled at her; the shame of that grandmother's dressing down is still right there in her gut, waiting for a chance to bubble up. "And, uh..." she sets aside the nutrient bars she can no longer afford and holds out the few that remain. "These. B'vakashah."

"Sorry, motek, prices went up last cycle. Fifteen for the filter now." The vollie's shoulders droop. "It's the mesh – it can't be reclaimed. We're trying to find a donor to cover it, but..."

Limor nods; it's not their fault. She pushes a few more away, feeling her guts tighten as she does. "This many, then."

The volunteer wraps the filter securely and processes the payment. "Bring your Ema to the kitchen, nu? Get some real food into you both."

"She doesn't like it."

"I know." The volunteer gestures helplessly at the tiny stack of nutrient bars.

2

"I'll try," Limor lies. She folds the small parcel into her scarf and walks out, farewelled by the sensor's beep.

***

Sub-T is waking up. People are stirring in their bedrolls; some walk to the charity kitchen, where the prayer service is held. The Gemaḥ officially runs it as non-denominational, but since most of the refugees (Limor included) and the charity volunteers are Jewish, it leans heavily that way.

"They want you there to make themselves feel good," Em says on her more coherent days. "They'll never really accept you, so why bother?"

Limor isn't sure about that, but then again there are all those prayers, chanted in ancient Ivrit. They can be hard to follow, even with modern Ivrit as Limor's mother tongue. And she isn't sure she has anything to say to Hashem, so she doesn't go, for all the rabbi said that it was less about God and more about community. She thinks about it, though; sometimes there's a free breakfast afterwards. And always, at least a sip of mayim ḥayim, for saying amen to the brakha. She knows how to do that much, if nothing else.

If only Em weren't so proud. They aren't starving, anyway, not quite. Not usually. A few years back, when she was still little enough to be tempted by cake, she went. The way Em yelled and shook her until her teeth rattled was enough to convince her that it wasn't worth it. Somehow Em always knew. It made Limor wonder if she wasn't really one of the mind-reading witches from the stories Em told to scare her when she was little. But no, the Kohenot are only Up-station, not down here.

Walking the maze of shipping container homes and stinking latrine areas, Limor knows everyone down here at least by sight. Some nod or wave as she passes and some ignore her, but that's to be expected. Everyone is stuck down here, like her, except for the volunteers, and not everyone is cheerful about it.

She rounds a corner and nearly bumps into Matt and a couple of his friends. Matt's... not a friend exactly, but he's her age and mostly all right. Kids and teens are fairly scarce in Sub-T, with birth control mandated from Up-station, so she can't be too choosy. Sometimes, when Limor thinks about that, she wishes she had the energy to be angry. At any rate, Matt's never sneered at her about Em, which counts for more than Limor wants to admit. It's not Em's fault, what happened to her, but not everyone sees it that way.

When Matt gestures silence at Limor, she follows his line of sight.

3

There's an Up-station stranger, slight of build and on the shorter side of average, swaggering with a confidence that seems naive. His clothes look expensive, despite their simplicity – black stretchy trousers and a shirt with a sporting logo and colourful shoes. His long brown hair, a few shades darker than his skin, is wound into a loose knot. His datapad is obvious in his back pocket; big mistake down here.

"My mark," Matt mouths, and prowls off before Limor can point out that this might be a new vollie, off-limits. He's going to get himself into all sorts of trouble. Grinding her teeth, she trails after him, hoping to whisper a discreet reminder.

But she's too late. He's already making a move, his friends backing him up. They likely planned this minutes before, one nagging for creds with a battered handheld scanner and the other following, footsteps loud enough to unsettle the mark and mask Matt's movements. Oldest trick in the book, but it still works on the right target.

Limor tries to catch up. She has to look out for Matt, who's being impulsive. She leaps when Matt does, sure she can yank him off the stranger's back. But there's nothing in that space when she lands, stumbling a little but still on her feet. The person has plucked Matt out of the air and Limor turns in time to see him deposit Matt gently in the gutter. Matt's cronies are already there, looking as startled as Limor feels.

A savta shakes Matt by the shoulders, her gnarled fingers gripping tightly. She scolds Matt in shrill, rapid-fire Ivrit, which he isn't fluent in, but he likely catches the concepts of respect and loving the foreigner. Normally Limor would take over, but she's distracted by the stranger, who winks at her, and moves on through the crowd as if nothing happened.

Limor follows.

***

His destination is the Membrane, which Limor usually avoids, but curiosity has got the better of her. The grey zone around the Up-station elevators always crawls with security. The guards are twice her size; obviously grown planet-side – Mainlanders. Limor keeps to the shadows. She hasn't forgotten what it was like when she and Em first arrived. They were just as unwanted then as they are now, that final ship of refugees, but there was nowhere else to go; they'd already been turned away from the Mainland, the last habitable planet in the system.

The guards don't carry guns. Limor hasn't seen one of those since...for a long time. Only small batons that can reboot a neural implant on their lowest settings, and electrocute a person to death on their highest, with plenty of pain settings in between for people without implants, like Limor. She's never felt it, having mastered the art of making herself small and invisible, but the images of other refugees writhing in pain are seared into her memory. One time, it was Em, but Limor tries not to think about that, the first time she had to be her mother's mother, the beginning of the downward spiral.

The stranger enters a makeshift building Limor's never seen before. These people must have somehow got permission to build here because Up-station space is impossible to get, every centimetre already allocated to a purpose. The guards wouldn't just be standing by otherwise. A sign over the doorway is emblazoned with letters in a script Limor can't read.

Limor's mind is a bubbling stew of curiosity, fear, and anger at Sub-T's meagre space being encroached. Not that any refugee would settle so close to the Membrane, but...

Like most public Sub-T buildings, there's no roof. Not as though the rain gets in down here, and it helps with air flow. The walls are pretty sturdy. Tucking her shopping tighter into the scarf tied to her back, Limor begins to climb. She's grown up climbing shipping crates and decommed shuttles for fun, so she's adept at finding hand and toe holds, and she soon reaches the top and pokes her head over cautiously.

About fifteen people are milling around, some chatting quietly, others stretching or shadow boxing. There's a mix of people, with a range of skin tones, some different gender markers, and around half have a visible neural implant on the side of their heads. The others are so gorgeous they have to be modded, not a None like Limor, too poor for an implant, let alone genetic modifications. She stares at them, suddenly conscious of her unremarkable features and lank hair.

The stranger – who Limor notices is 'planted –emerges from a closed-off area. Immediately, the others form a line and bow to him as he approaches. He's wearing the same outfit as the others: loose white trousers and jacket, fastened with a belt. A black one. Like a karate uniform, Limor remembers from a vid that used to play on the public screen, back when it was still working. But that vid was all about punching and kicking and these people, after they've jogged around the mats for a few minutes, are tumbling and wrestling.

She hunkers down and watches, rapt, as they take turns flipping each other over. The instructor demonstrates flipping a person twice their size over, back slapping audibly against the mats. No wonder he wasn't worried about strolling through Sub-T with his tech on display. Still, she can't help but wonder how they got permission for this, with the anti-militia laws and all.

When the class wraps up, Limor's muscles are cramping and she begins to climb down, quiet and reluctant.

"Enjoyed the show?"

Limor whirls around. It's the instructor, still in his uniform. Barefoot, as she is, he's the same height as Limor, who might yet grow some more.

"I, uh, sorry, I," she stammers.

"I'll let you off this time." He smiles. "I'm Zeke, and it's my dojo. You want a beam with course details?"

"Got no pad."

"Oh." His face falls.

"Got no creds for classes either." Limor shrugs and turns. "Thanks anyway."

***

Anyway, she's busy, looking after Em and getting the water purifier fixed – like any refurb, it takes fiddling – and scrounging more food. She even asks Em if she wants to go to the kitchen for a meal, but Em growls at her. Matt rolls his eyes when she stumbles over her words to ask and buys her a few packets of instant noodles. More than he can afford, she's sure, but she needs to feed Em. She'll make it up to him when things even out. It'll only be a couple more cycles, if Em's careful with her supply. Or her dealer takes pity on her.

Still, a few days later Limor finds herself perched at the top of the dojo's wall again. Her muscles twitch as she watches, as though they're yearning to do the movements. The sound of rain is clearer here; it's soothing and adds rhythm to their training. This time, she creeps down before the class ends. At home, she tries to move her body the way they do, but there isn't enough space and Em yells at her to stop thumping.

***

She goes back. And again. She has a favourite spot on the wall now. If Zeke notices her again, he makes no sign of it.

After some weeks of this, it's a routine, and maybe Limor gets complacent, or maybe she's just unlucky.

"Hey!" a guard calls from below.

Limor freezes. She can't risk tangling with guards. But staying here will only make things worse. Her heart pounds in her mouth.

Instructor and students stop and look up. Zeke looks annoyed more than anything, but one the students puts her hand on his shoulder. She beckons to Limor. Only when Limor has started climbing down the inside of the wall does she run for the door. She's either calling off the guards or Limor is in extremely deep shit.

By the time Limor has reached the ground, Zeke's expression is impressed. "You made that look easy, like a spider monkey," he says.

"A what?"

His face flickers, like it did the first time they spoke to Limor. "An old Earth creature, a primate like us. They're good at climbing. And gangly, like you."

"Oh. Uh, thanks for the help. I should go." She turns towards the door.

"Actually, I told the guards that you were staying." The woman who'd welcomed her in had returned. She's tall and willowy, with light brown skin not unlike Limor's. As she speaks, she turns to smile at Limor. One side of her head is shaved, showing off her neural implant and the intricate tattoos around it. Zeke is introducing her as Adi when sirens ring in Limor's mind.

Those tattoos aren't just for decoration; at their centre is a cursive 'ayin. Stylised to look like a raindrop, it's the compulsory branding for a Kohenet; mind-reader; witch. Most people shield Kohenet telepathy with their implants, or datapads if they're modded. Limor has neither. That means Adi can read everything she's thinking, all her secrets. Limor takes a step back, stumbling over her own feet.

"Hey now," Zeke says. "Kohenot don't *really* eat children, y'know."

"Easy for you to say," Limor mumbles. "*You're* protected."

Zeke clicks his tongue. "I don't need protection from one of the most vulnerable groups in our society." The words sound practised, as though he's had to say them often. The other students disperse toward the change rooms, unruffled by the scene like they've already heard it a thousand times.

"Up there, at least." Adi looks towards the station proper, then fixes unblinking brown eyes on Limor's face. If she's hurt by Limor's comment, she doesn't show it.

Limor's heart twists in an unfamiliar direction. Adi's expression is unlike the condescending sympathy she's most used to from citizens, when there's attention on her at all. Was it a moment of shared understanding? She's never given much thought to how Kohenot must chafe against surveillance. At least down here no one is monitoring her every thought, making sure she's not snooping. "I'm sorry," she whispers.

"So am I," Adi says. She's a fully grown adult, but the way she speaks makes Limor feel like she's not just a kid. It's another difference between

Adi and the other Up-station folk Limor has encountered.

"For what?"

Adi gestures in an up-and-down motion, miming the station. "For how things are."

A tense silence descends, broken by Limor. "Please teach me," she says to Zeke and Adi. "I don't have creds but I could clean, or do errands, or..." She's not foolish enough to think that martial arts might save her from armed guards, but she can think of so many circumstances where this might help.

Zeke scratches his head. "Adi, you've been saying ages that you wanted to learn how to teach. If you want to show the kid a few things I won't object."

Adi's brow furrows, then clears. "OK, let me show you some basic forms and then we'll drill one of them."

There are take downs and grips and sweeps and – Limor's head starts to spin. Zeke reappears, dressed in a lycra suit that must be for going outside in the rain. "Don't overwhelm her, motek," he says.

"Right! I, uh, was trying to give an overview."

He ducks his head gracefully. "Give it time. Start with something fun."

Adi nods. "Right. Uh, well ... a sweep from guard?"

"Yofi, then she learns guard too."

"What's guard?" Limor asks.

"It's how you defend yourself when you're on the bottom. Like this." She wraps her legs around Limor, who's kneeling on the mats. "If you're on your back, it's your basic defence. You try." She scoots off to give Limor space. "Nice and tight, good. Pull me in with your knees. Now, grab my lapel..."

It takes a few tries before Limor gets the physics of it, but once she does, she can flip Adi over and clamber onto her belly in one movement, even though Adi must be at least twenty kilos heavier than her. She laughs, exhilarated.

"See? OK, that's enough. I'll be late for tefilla if I don't go soon."

She's been keeping Adi from going outside, where she can be in the holy rain and connect with Hashem. Kohenot take it especially seriously, Limor remembers, and she's been selfish, and she needs to check on Em, and... "Sorry."

"No, don't be! I have to manage my own time. Come a couple of times a week and watch the class, OK? I'm sure Zeke won't mind."

***

Limor settles into a rhythm over the next few weeks and months. Adi rejects Limor's offers to clean the dojo; apparently everyone takes turns with that. Limor knows she's a charity case but she doesn't care, she wants to learn so desperately. She takes the protein bars Adi offers her after each session with a quiet thanks.

The moves are starting to make sense to her body; Adi makes her repeat them until they flow, and Limor can't help but notice Adi growing more confident as a teacher, hesitating less as she decides what to demonstrate next. Zeke stops by and corrects both of them sometimes, staying longer and longer as Limor's technique improves. At home, she drills quietly while Em sleeps. After a few weeks, she can roll, forwards and backwards, without a sound. In the dojo mirror, she's surprised to see muscle definition on her shoulders. She's always been thin and wiry, but this is new.

One time she overhears Zeke say something about how he wishes Limor could compete. Adi turns away without speaking.

The other students are polite and friendly, but distant. Most of them go outside after class. In bits and pieces, she discovers that for some of them, being in the rain is a spiritual experience, while for others it's fun or relaxing; Limor doesn't quite understand any of it, and doesn't dare let herself want to find out. Adi seems to be the most religious, but she's not pushy about it like some of the volunteers.

Limor never talks to Adi about Em, or anything about her life, and Adi never asks. When Adi calls time, Limor slips back to her reality. No one notices if she's gone for a couple of hours. Except Em. Limor lies, gives excuses, and makes sure to go to different sessions so there isn't too much of a pattern. She knows Em won't understand, and her mother is distracted, anyway. Supply issues or something. Secrets everywhere.

***

There's a jolt through Limor's shoulder as she walks home. She's not hyper-aware like Zeke; she's tired and sore and wrapped in her thoughts and doesn't hear Matt's barefooted steps until it's too late. "Think you're too good for us now?" He shoves her again.

"No different'n I've been." Limor tries to shrink back into herself, become invisible, but it's too late for that.

Matt follows. "You've been hanging with those Up-station snobs. Getting airs, and rains."

"Just training a bit, right here in Sub-T. 'Sno different'n having breakfast at the kitchen. No rain."

9

"Dunno about that. That Zeke, I heard he's a dissident. And a Kohenet? You're gonna regret tangling with Up-station folks, especially that sort."

Limor laughs despite herself, not bothering to hide her scorn, even though it feels petty. "These folks? All they do is train and go outside. They're just cruising. Not that Kohenot can do much even if they want to. Those bugged implants, remember?"

Matt crosses his arms. "Maybe. Still, you should stay away from them. Nobody trains that hard if they aren't spoiling for a fight."

She scowls upwards, then at Matt. "You saying you wouldn't fight if you had the chance?"

"That's a pretty big if."

Limor chews her lip. Em would agree with him. Keep your head down, don't cause trouble. And she's good at that, but somehow that's not enough anymore. If airs and rains means she wishes she could feel the holy rain, or just walk free anywhere, or even – the thought comes to her in the smallest of whispers – have a baby one day, maybe she does have them, even if Adi and Zeke never meant to share even that shred of hope.

Matt laughs at her. "Don't look so serious. Show me a move, aye?"

"No, I'm not ready, I–"

Still laughing, still playing, he grabs her shirt. "Go on, or I'll know you're snobbing it up."

Limor isn't in the mood to play. She grabs his wrist with both hands and pulls, fast enough to surprise him, and yanks him down, leaning forwards like she's been taught so he ends up flipped over on his back. Still holding his wrist, she throws one leg over his chest and the other over his neck. She arches. In seconds, he screams – he doesn't know about tapping – and she releases him.

"Hot," he says as he scrambles up.

"Fuck off."

"Seriously. Dunno what you want to be ready for but I reckon you are."

Limor isn't sure either. Her ideas haven't finished forming yet, but she knows in her bones that she's more of a dissident than Zeke, if not Adi, who at least thinks about things. Has to. "Really, I'm not, you let me do that. I just started."

Matt shakes his head. "Can I come too?"

She remembers the noodles. "I'll ask."

***

10

But she doesn't. There's no way she can make it to training today. Em hasn't heard from her dealer for ... days? Weeks? Limor would venture out to try to find out what's happened to him if Em didn't need her constantly. Instead she mashes a nutrient bar into some water to make a paste and spoons it into her mother's mouth, hoping against hope Em doesn't puke it up. Wipes sweat off her face. There's no chance of getting her to the latrine in time; the towels Limor used to line her bed will have to suffice. She knows what to do; she's done it before and got through it more times than she can count.

She has no way to contact Adi, so she gets on with it, drilling in her mind while her body cares for her shaking mother. They won't miss her; everyone skips sometimes. Things happen. But somehow she doesn't think the happy, carefree students are ever doing this. And it feels ungrateful to skip when she's not paying them. At least they'll be able to go straight outside today, instead of her slowing them down.

She's lost track of time when there's a knock on the door. It reverbs through the shelter and Em groans.

Limor says, "I'll check if it's him."

But it's not. It's Adi, wearing a black hooded coat that's probably effective against the cold, but looks out of place down here. She's much too polite to say anything but she can't hide the flicker of disgust as Limor slips out the door and closes it behind her, aware of the stench wafting out. "We were worried," Adi says. "And I thought maybe I should meet your Ema anyway."

"That's not a good idea." Belatedly, she tries to soften it. "At least, not today."

"What's wrong?"

"She's sick. Gotta go. Sorry. Thanks for checking."

Adi places a gentle hand on Limor's shoulder. "Maybe I can help?"

Limor shakes her head vigorously and opens the door again. People are going to notice soon, start talking.

But Adi shamelessly looks over Limor's head into the shelter. "That woman needs medical care, not a child looking after her."

"Go away." For a second Limor doesn't care that Adi might get angry and stop teaching her, but then her heart sinks. "Please."

Adi is already turning away, shoulders set squarely. "I am going, to find a doctor."

"Got no creds for that."

"I'll pay for it." She gestures towards the door. "Don't waste time arguing, go back to your Ema."

Limor's heart is racing, but it's slow compared to Em's. Limor tries in vain to coax her to breathe deeply. The bed is drenched with sweat and urine. The thought of washing the sheets and recycling that water makes Limor want to cry but she can't, not now, not when Em needs her. She has to stay strong, always.

But then the door is opening and Adi is there with a Sub-T medic. At least it isn't some fancy doctor from Up-station. Em glares at Limor but she doesn't protest – she's too unwell to yell curses at anyone.

While Em's with the medic, Limor gets the sheets cleaned, and the rest of the shelter too. The medic's work is more effective than Limor's; Em's eyes have some light in them that Limor hasn't seen for a while. When she's settled back onto her pallet, Em says, "So you've got some fancy friends. They want you for a pet. A mascot. They'll forget you when they find another new shiny project."

"A thank you'd be nice for once." Limor stands, feeling taller than she used to; Em's eyes widen and Limor can tell she sees it too. "Going to train."

No more secrets.

***

She's only had a few days off, but everything hurts. Adi calls the session early and hands Limor a protein bar. "You want to talk about it?"

"Dunno." Limor shrugs and curls up small, savouring the snack. It tastes so much better than the cheap ones the Gemaḥ stocks. "Really appreciate what you did."

Adi chews her lip. "I never really realised, what it's like for you. I wish I could do more," she says. "Get you out of here."

Something in Limor snaps, surprising even her. "What, just me? Why? 'cause I have some talent for your sport?" She tries to keep the bitterness out of her voice, but she's failing. "M'grateful, really, but I..."

Adi's face crumples, but she says nothing.

Suddenly animated, Limor stands. "I can't abandon Em and I don't want to. She's only like this because of what happened to us, she's not trash to be salvaged. This is my home. These are my *people*."

"They're our people too–" Adi begins to say, startling as Zeke approaches and places a hand on her shoulder.

But that just makes Limor angrier. She interrupts, eyes on Zeke now. "And you. You come down here, take our space–"

"We were kicked out of our gym because of crackdowns on Kohenot–"

"And you're doing nothing, even less than Adi. What's your excuse?" She claps a hand over her mouth. "I'll... go."

"I think that would be best," Adi says, voice choked.

Limor runs.

***

"Back so soon?" Em asks. Her smug expression fades when she sees Limor's tear-stained face.

"You were right," Limor sobs. She's still wearing her borrowed uniform, she realises; the thought of having to return stings.

"Shh, it's OK," Em holds a thin arm out and Limor collapses against her, despite her mother's boniness. "You still did good even if it didn't last. You helped me. We'll get back to normal now."

It's the kindest thing Em has said to her for... well, a while. But to Limor, normal seems impossible. She's been pulled out of her world and back in so many times, she's dizzy. Deep in her belly, there's a force pushing for more, she's just not sure what to do with it anymore.

***

The next time Limor stops at the Gemaḥ, Adi is behind the counter, midway through volunteer training. Limor cringes, wishing more than anything that her invisibility skills were real magic, instead of clever camouflage. Too late to back out now, though. Adi's already seen her, and anyway, she needs food for her and Em, and noodles for Matt. Next time she'll be able to get veggies.

"Ring it up like this, motek." The older volunteer is showing Adi how to use the scanner.

Adi, however, is not giving it her full attention. Limor looks down at the counter, trying to avoid eye contact; she can see Adi is fishing in her pocket. Is she trying to pay for Limor's groceries?

No, she's waving a holo flyer at Limor. "I was hoping I'd get a chance to show you this. Is it OK? I can use a different vid, I just thought..."

Limor unrolls the flyer. A quickvid shows Limor putting Adi in an arm lock. The text, repeated in every language Limor's familiar with, offers free weekly classes and promises fun for all ages. And there's a little map of Zeke's dojo. A lump forms in Limor's throat. "S'perfect," she whispers. "Zeke's OK with it?"

A line is forming behind Limor. The volunteer snaps her fingers in front of Adi's face. Quick as a flash, Adi scans her own cred card to pay for Limor's groceries and begs leave to step aside for a second. "I wondered if you might like to be an assistant teacher? I'll probably need it, and a local connection would be best. And yes, Zeke's paying me a wage for this. You, too, if you want in."

The rain pounds above, clearer than usual. Must be a storm, but if Limor didn't know better she'd swear it was drums, or whispered prayers; she's not sure which. A portent of change, a beginning that feels more real than their last one. Limor takes a deep breath. She's ready. "Yes."

3.4 oz
R.K. KALAW

There's a certain kind of magic that we not-quite-immigrants learned, we in-between people without Green Card or Citizenship, those of tenuous status and home.

This is what you show, and this is what you hide, to keep people comfortable around you. This is how you dress, and this is how you speak, and this is what you carry, so you won't be flagged at the airport. Nothing of yours can exceed 3.4 oz.

My older sister, my Ate, taught me the compliance magic, the "3.4 cram" or the "palit-siksik," over the course of one frantic night. She still worked in the US, then. This was long before she got sick, when she was still in peak form, prime Domineering Raging Bitch.

Six hours before my morning flight, my Ate Kristine held me hostage in the cramped, dinky bathroom of her apartment, and forced me to master the magic. It was already two am. Krissy shared the one-bedroom with two other Filipinas, which was the only reason we were hissing at a whisper instead of screaming at each other. The bathroom walls were so thin that you could hear a mouse floss.

"Come on. Try it again, MoMo." Krissy was goading me. She knew I hated that nickname for Ramona, the name people back home still used. MoMo was fine, for a toddler or terrier. At each college I'd started at, in Jersey then Boston then Philly, I'd told everyone to call me "Moe."

"I'm done," I said. "I'm taking a break."

Krissy sighed, her special I'm-so-patient-with-your-fuck-ups sigh. "No breaks. I told you to practice this shit a week ago, MoMo."

"I've been practicing for the last fucking month."

"*Hey*. Don't you start lying to me."

"*Hey*," I said, mimicking her tone. "You still don't get it. Just 'cause things are easy for *you*, doesn't mean they're easy for *me*."

"Don't whine and drag this out. That only works on Mom. Some of us have to work tomorrow."

"And you wonder why I never visit."

Ate Krissy shoved me forward, and my hip bones banged the

bathroom counter. In a few hours, I'd have bruises. Krissy's roommates thought she was all sweetness and light, baking them banana bread, and teaching them how to do a razor-sharp winged eyeliner. They didn't know. My Ate was only sweet to people she didn't give a shit about. She kept three rows of razor wire around her heart, and she only loved a few people. But when she loved you, she owned you.

"I can't refund my ticket," I said quietly, grimacing down at the counter. I didn't rub at where my bruises would be, because I never showed my sister where she'd hurt me. I wanted to cry, not because I was fried and exhausted, or because I was afraid of Krissy, but because her judgment was thick in the room, sucking out all my life and air.

I didn't need to look at Krissy's eyes in the mirror. Look up, she was thinking. Look at me. You need to step up. You need to dress better. You need to stop hiding. You need to talk to people like a normal human being.

"I don't care if you can't refund your ticket," said Krissy. "Either I'm driving you to the airport, or I'm driving you to the bus station."

I laughed, because it was the only way I could fight back. "Fuck you."

"You need this," she said, not in English or Tagalog, but in Cebuano. "You need this magic. To keep you safe. So learn it." When she broke out the pure Cebuano with me, she was channeling my Mom's mom, and I was on very thin ice.

She was shorter than me, but she stared me down. "You're not leaving till I let you leave."

***

I didn't know if Krissy's guidance helped or hindered me. All I knew was that I wanted to escape her.

The bathroom counter was sticky with my prior attempts to pour myself into TSA-compliant 3.4 ounce plastic bottles. This was supposed to be simple shit. The magic would let me temporarily ditch my personal baggage. High, volatile emotions were dangerous—they could get you sent to Secondary Screening, or worse. The new administration couldn't tell a raging radical from an angsty fuck-up. I'd found that out the hard way.

The latest body scanners screened for more than bombs and guns and contraband. They tried to get into your head by analyzing whiffs of complex pheromones, the stress chemicals in sweat and skin, seeking the markers of suspicion. Our magic countered this by bottling everything in you and setting it aside, safe from scrutiny.

We had planned out what I could fit into a dinky 1 quart Ziploc bag:

3.4 oz of shampoo: to pour out my rage.

3.4 oz of conditioner: to pour out my fear of them.

3.0 oz of face wash: to drain my hate. *Stop staring. Stop asking where I'm from.*

1.0 oz sunblock: to drain despair. *I'm so goddamned tired, just let me go home. Everyone I love is there.*

0.7 oz cream concealer: to drain desperation. *I'll never go back, I'm going to stay. They can't take this life away from me. Everyone I love is here.*

1.0 oz Sticky Rice matte pomade: just because. *This is the only stuff that spikes my hair just right, and the wasted space will piss Ate Krissy off.*

Krissy stood behind me, grabbing my wrists so my hands wouldn't shake, though that made me shake worse. Having her there worked me up. I exploded several more plastic bottles, before I got my shampoo-rage to go down and stay down. Slowly, I managed the others. Each bottle was a victory against her.

Krissy didn't tell me I'd done a good job, because perfection was what she expected of me. "You won't be flagged again," Krissy said. She let go of my wrists. She didn't hug me or touch me again. She leaned on the bathroom counter, hands shaking, as if she'd done all the work.

There was a glob of sunblock in her hair, but I didn't tell her about it. "I'll clean up here," she said. "Wash your face off and get some sleep, so you don't look like shit in line. Christ, MoMo. I shouldn't have to tell you this. What would you do, without me around?"

She knew about her diagnosis, even then. I'd never forgive her for that.

***

I wondered why Krissy stopped our Skype calls. She didn't want me to see her face.

Ate Krissy hid her sickness for as long as she could before going back to Manila, so our parents could take care of her. There wasn't much they could do, by then, aside from keeping her comfortable. By the time Mom gave me The Call, Krissy was mostly gone, semi-comatose and nonverbal, barely responsive to light or pain.

I drained my savings to book the ticket home, to Manila and back again. My visa was still valid, but my re-entry wasn't guaranteed. They could find a reason, any reason, to lock me out of the country. I'd spent years here, building a new life brick by brick, remaking myself piece by piece. Still, I'd risk it all. It was worth holding Krissy's hand again, while it was still warm.

***

International travel was another level of risk. Our puny, palit-siksik magic could only shield me so much.

I knew what would happen, on re-entry. The same thing that had happened when I'd flown to Montreal for Spring Break. I'd stand in front the Immigration Officer's fortified cubicle. It'd be a different face through the glass, but they'd have the same eyes, staring me down like I was an insect, as they leafed through my stack of supporting documentation. Maybe they'd use the same ruse, cheerfully say someone was coming to help me with my bags, when they meant I was being sequestered to Secondary Screening. There'd be a room full of scared, befuddled brown people there, from profile countries. The cell signal would be blocked.

Krissy had lost her shit trying to get a hold of me, waiting to pick me up. When I got my phone back, there were over fifty missed calls and texts. I wished I hadn't deleted her angry voice mails, ripping me a new asshole in three languages.

Today, I inched forward through the Immigration line, knowing Krissy wasn't waiting for me on the other side. They could really deport me, now. There was no death certificate for Krissy, no funeral notice, and I couldn't justify this trip. But maybe it wouldn't matter to them, either way.

In Secondary, they'd ask me the same questions, over and over, seeing if I'd crack. This time, when they confiscated my phone, they'd find a different set of pictures. Not me half passed-out at a Montreal bar, still knocking down drinks to force myself to enjoy the party. They'd see shots of yellow roses, a hospital room packed with them. Krissy's high school friends, her old barkada, had come by with yellow bouquets, because it was her favorite color. Even her enemies and her exes had brought golden roses.

In Secondary, when they cloned my phone, they'd dig up the two files I'd deleted. The first was a video Mom covertly took of me singing to Krissy. It was the childhood Taglish-Cebuano song we'd made up to mock our poor overworked Yaya Wilma, about her getting eaten by a goat from the slippers up, complete with the appropriate sound effects. I couldn't get through the whole song, not while watching Krissy like that.

The second deleted file was taken after Mom left, when Krissy and I were alone. I hadn't wanted any pictures of my Ate's face, with her eyes cracked open to slivers of white. Instead, I'd taken a shot of my hand around hers, avoiding her IV and the heart monitor capped to her finger. Her palms weren't warm and comforting, but unpleasantly clammy.

Afterwards, I'd leaned in to whisper to Krissy. If coma patients could still hear things, I'd get the last word in, finally. She couldn't tell me how I should feel.

"Just lie there, bitch," I'd said. "You can do better. You're not trying hard enough. You're not leaving till I let you leave."

***

The Immigration odds were stacked against me, this trip. I was carrying too much with me. Too much to cram into a sealed quart Ziploc.

Still, I crossed my first border, the yellow strip you waited behind, before you were next in line. This Immigration Officer looked bored, tired, and indifferent. He flipped through the documents I handed him, bank statements, old transcripts, past proof of employment. He frowned. I was in the dangerous grey area between statuses, not student or worker or tourist.

When directed, I took off my cap and looked up for the identification photo. I mashed my fingers into the scanner. It was rumored they took covert chemical readings here, too. Was I clear? Had I emptied myself enough?

***

The night before my flight back, I had done the magic alone, without Krissy holding my wrists, or her voice hissing in my ear. There was a lot more counter space in the big blue-tiled guest bathroom at my parent's. So old Yaya Wilma wouldn't have to clean up after me, I'd mopped up my spills and exploding emotions with fluffy bath towels. I couldn't keep things down, or pour them out. Krissy was still in the hospital. It was killing me to stay. It was killing me to leave her.

You could drink your feelings away, they said. From the back of our liquor cabinet, I'd grabbed the lambanog. It was home-brew made by a distant cousin's family, sketchily packaged in empty Gilbey's Gin bottles. They sent us some every Christmas, and my folks politely stored it out of sight, too low-brow for their tastes. Krissy had facilitated my first hangover at sixteen, on New Years, by pouring lambanog into my Coke when the parents weren't watching.

I'd drunk, just short of getting shit-faced, because my flight was in the early am. On a whim, I'd filled my mouth with lambanog, and spat my grief out into my glass. The liquor had held me in. I'd poured my grief out into empty two-Liter plastic Coke bottles, three, then four, then five of them, over forty fluid ounces. My mouth burned, by the time I was done.

19

I was still drunk when I'd boarded my plane at NAIA airport, but I was peaceful and hollow.

***

I left my fingers on the Immigration scanner, waiting for the green light that showed their readings had been taken. I was pushing the limits of the magic, stowing that much sentiment in my suitcase.

Whatever feelings you packaged for smooth travel only left you temporarily. You had to keep them tethered near you. I didn't know how far I could stretch the leash, piling illegal liquor and dangerous, flammable sorrow into my checked luggage.

The bright, sharp, seething parts of me were sealed in those plastic Coke bottles. The bulk of my grief. My rage and fear and love and hate and homesickness.

The hand scanner was fighting to read me. I answered the Officer's curt questions without emotion, maintaining eye contact. My feet didn't shuffle, and my voice didn't shake. My home accent didn't come out strong and thick, like it did when I was agitated.

Their scanner light went green. It read me as compliant. Safe enough to allow in. The agent waved me through. He had to wave twice, before it registered with me.

At the luggage carousel, I reunited myself with my heavy, roiling emotions. They had yet to sink back into me, and be reabsorbed. My chaotic feelings weren't contraband. They couldn't be stolen, or left behind, or confiscated by anyone, and that was good. I wanted them with me, my love and grief most of all.

I wheeled my luggage to the Customs checkpoint.

"Anything to declare?" they asked.

"Nothing," I said, and they let me walk past them.

IN THE BACKGROUND
BARBARA KRASNOFF

"Have you heard the latest?"

Sharah sat in holding, a partially finished cup of over-milked and over-sugared coffee in one hand, feeling tired and not a little grumpy. Her 1940s-era girdle was so tight that she felt as if she needed to piss every half hour, and she dreaded the moment she'd have to put those damned high heels back on. She shook her head and took a moment to stare around the room.

"Holding" was the place where the background players (also known as extras) for the popular video show *Rosie the Romantic Riveter* were kept out of the way when they weren't on set. The room was filled with about 60 people dressed in various 1940s-era costumes who had been ushered into holding about 6:30 a.m. after two hours of costume fittings, hair stylings and make-up. It was now 2 p.m. and they were still there, leaving only for brief visits to the bathroom.

As a result, what had started out as neat rows of folding chairs and a carefully arranged snack table was now a chaotic mess. The chairs had been shifted around by people who wanted to face each other in groups, or who needed footrests or improvised tables. Empty paper plates and coffee cups lay strewn around the floor along with several dozen pairs of era-appropriate but uncomfortable high-heeled shoes.

The backgrounders – women in formal dresses and men in tuxes, along with "waiters" and "cigarette girls" in appropriate attire – sat reading, chatting, knitting, playing cards, or chewing on stale pastry from the snack table. Occasionally an assistant director came in to make an announcement, ask for quiet, or choose one or two backgrounders, and then disappeared again. Makeup artists occasionally wandered the room, checking to see if anyone's makeup or hair needed touching up.

"What's the latest?" asked George, a distinguished-looking 50-something in a tux who was part of Sharah's small group of acquaintances, and who had just finished complaining that his bow tie was more uncomfortable than the women's high heels. ("And I should know," he added. "I spent years as a drag queen in the East Village until my voice

21

gave out....")

"They're going to put the word 'illegitimate' back on the birth certificates of babies born to unmarried girls," said Jill, a blonde young woman wearing a WAC uniform, bright red lipstick and sensible shoes, which Sharah envied immensely. "Bastards."

"Shhh!" Melissa was a gray-haired woman somewhere in her 60s who was, like Sharah, dressed in an appropriately upscale dress. She looked around nervously. "We shouldn't talk about things like that," she whispered. "They may be recording." She could have been talking about the video crew on set next door, or about the security cameras set into two corners of the large room. Or both.

"So we'll just have to replay 'Blossoms in the Dust,'" George said. When nobody reacted, he shook his head in disgust. "Doesn't anyone here know their classic films? It starred Greer Garson and Walter Pidgeon. Biopic about the woman who got the word 'illegitimate' struck off birth certificates in Texas."

"Well, it's about to be struck on again," said Jill. "They're going to add it for all children born within the last five years. And there's rumors that they're also going to be adding a code for mixed-race children as well – whatever the hell mixed-race means these days."

She deliberately looked away from Sharah, who didn't say anything.

Sharah often didn't say anything. She had rent to pay and a mother and a kid to support, and her unemployment from her last full-time job ran out last year. Even fast-food jobs were hard to come by these days, so when a friend sent her a notice about a casting company that was looking for backgrounders, she had grabbed the chance for the freelance gigs with both hands.

That was six months ago, and since then, the work had been pretty steady. Because Sharah resembled her Russian mother more than her Jamaican father, she was able to apply for productions that needed people with an ethnic look ("ethnic" these days being a polite way of saying "stereotype"), such as a wealthy Jewish matron, an overdressed Italian mafia mother, a furtive Hispanic refugee, or an exotic Harlem showgirl. She could also melt into crowds, so she was a good general fit. And she was medium height, kept herself slim despite her 40-something years, and had developed a reputation for paying attention to directions and not caring what she was dressed like as long as they paid her.

Today Sharah was playing the part of an anonymous attendee at a high-class New York nightclub. *Rosie the Romantic Riveter* was a corporate-funded historical soaper whose 15-minute episodes were released every day at noon for download by thousands of eager fans. It took place in New York City during World War II and had a storyline that emphasized, along with Rosie's various trials and tribulations, an America where everyone worked toward the common good through patriotism and sacrifice. It was crap, of course, but popular crap. And it paid well, even if you were only a backgrounder.

A plump young woman with purple hair, one of the assistant directors, ran in and yelled, "Quiet please! We'll be calling you in soon, but meanwhile, remember that sound bleeds over from this room into the set, so keep your voices down!"

The cacophony of voices softened for a few minutes.

"What's *their* problem?" Jill whispered, looking over Sharah's shoulder. Sharah turned around – a group of young men in their 20s dressed as waiters were whispering angrily to one another. "I'm gonna complain!" one said in a louder voice, and his friends immediately hushed him.

"They're just idiots," George said. "They started a multiplayer game on their phones, and then realized that their cameras weren't on."

"Didn't they read the directions?" Sharah asked, incredulous. Everyone was allowed to bring their phones – in fact, the Location Safety Law of 2020 required all citizens to carry one at all times with the GPS turned on so that they could be tracked by authorities "in case of emergency." However, because Rosie's storyline was kept a strict secret, the production had gotten special permission to remotely turn off all phone cameras in the building so people couldn't take pictures of the set or the costumes.

"I *said* they were idiots," George shrugged.

"Ladies and gentlemen!" the assistant director had returned. "Please! I have an announcement."

She looked around the room. "I'm sorry this is taking so long. We're nearly set up, so we'll be calling you in very shortly." She ran back out of the room.

"We're gonna be here forever," Jill groused. "And I had a date tonight."

"It's because they had to make last-minute story changes," Melissa whispered. She was a fan of the series and loved being on the inside; she talked to the crew every chance she got. "Rosie is going to have a new love interest. One of the makeup artists told me. The mechanic is going to die off-camera in a factory accident and Rosie is going to start dating a Russian soldier."

"Why?" Sharah asked. "What was wrong with the mechanic? He was a good-looking kid."

23

Jill leaned forward. "I heard that, in the last episode, the actor who played the mechanic emphasized the word 'resist' too much," she whispered. "The President watches the series and complained."

"That can't be it!" Melissa hissed. "He wouldn't do something like that!"

The others ignored her. "But the director must have noticed it. Why didn't he do a retake?" Sharah asked.

"Smithson? He's in such a hurry to meet his schedule, he's always missing stuff," Melissa said scornfully. "He can weasel out of almost anything. He probably convinced the higher-ups that he was in the bathroom, or in edit, or something."

"Takes talent," George said. "To be so good at pushing the responsibility for mistakes onto other people."

The assistant director came in. "Okay everyone, please be quiet!" she yelled, and waited a moment. "Everyone at tables 1-9, please come on set. Tables 1-9 only!"

"That's us," George said to Sharah.

"Yup." Sharah stood, drained her coffee cup, put it under her chair, and grabbed the small gold clutch bag that she'd been issued. She pushed her feet into her high heels and tottered toward the door (it always took her a few minutes to get used to wearing those damned things), along with George and about 40 other men and women.

They walked in an uneven line down a badly-painted hallway, through two heavy black curtains, and onto the set of what was supposed to be the Bluebird Nightclub. At the far end of the spacious room was a stage where musicians sat sucking on cans of soda and staring sourly at the incoming backgrounders. Behind them, a backdrop was decorated with two crossed American flags and a photo of FDR.

In front of the stage was a large cleared area where the floor show and dancing took place. On either side of the space were two rows of round tables where the club's "audience" sat. Each table was littered with a careful selection of fake alcoholic drinks, plates of half-eaten desserts, and ashtrays. There was also a single row of tables opposite the stage to indicate the edge of the dance floor and, when the cameras were placed behind them, to give the impression of more of an audience than the set really held.

Both Sharah and George had been assigned to table 3, along with two other couples. Table 3 was in the second row of tables on the left side of the stage, just behind the table where the actors playing Rosie and her friend Charlotte sat. Sharah liked sitting at table 3; she got to watch the director and the actors work without having to do much herself. It was a lot more interesting than sitting at one of the tables where you just pretended to be having fun without having anything to do or see.

The actors were sitting at their table now, while Smithson, a large, slightly overweight man with thinning blond hair, conferred with them in a low voice. Camera and lighting operators fussed with their equipment and assistants checked the fake food on the tables, while other backgrounders shuffled to their assigned places. Young men in waiters' uniforms leaned against the wall and two young women in abbreviated outfits fussed with trays full of the herbal cigarettes that were used in the place of real ones.

Sharah settled into her seat and put the clutch next to her plate. George sat to her left, in the chair closest to the table occupied by the series stars.

"You!" Another of the assistant directors, a tall young man with a thin, worried face, pointed to George, who obediently looked up. "The director said he wanted some movement behind the actors. He wants you to light a cigarette just after the band starts to play and wave it around, almost as if you were conducting the music."

"Like this?" George pulled one of the herbal cigarettes from a pack near him and, holding it like a stick, waved it around.

"No. Hold it between your fingers like you were smoking it and wave it around that way."

"Oh." George stuck the cigarette between his forefinger and middle finger and waved his hand around with the back of his hand outward so the cigarette was visible.

"That's it." The assistant strode over to another table. "Now, when music stops, I need you to stand up and walk over there…"

George grinned at Sharah. "It looks like we're going to be in shot."

She shrugged. "Is that important?"

"Well, it's fun, anyway. You can point yourself out to your friends in a couple of days when the episode airs." He considered her for a moment. "Of course, I understand if you want to stay off camera. Considering the type of nastiness being spread around these days."

You don't know the half of it, Sharah wanted to tell him. *The sour looks, the off-hand remarks. The loss of jobs. The fear.* She was tempted to say something, but then was interrupted by one of the assistants walking through, shouting, "Don't forget to turn off your phone notifications! Anything goes off during shooting and you're out of here!"

Sharah was fairly certain she had muted her phone, but just in case, she pulled it out of the clutch and checked. It was indeed muted – in fact, there was a text waiting for her from her mother. She took a moment to check it.

25

Norah next door said the Unfathered Infant Identification Act has been signed into law and that the baby will need new ID. What does that mean? Do we need to do something?

Shit. Sharah quickly typed in *Don't worry about it. We'll talk when I get home.* She put the phone back in the clutch, and took a breath, trying to calm herself. Then looked at George.

"You know," she said. "I'm starting to change my mind about some things. Staying in the background, I mean."

George raised an eyebrow. He looked like he was going to say more, when all the assistants started yelling for quiet.

"Okay, rehearsal!" Smithson called, and the assistants echoed, "Ready for rehearsal!"

The crewmembers, including a woman who had been carefully fixing the makeup of the actor who played Rosie, immediately left the set or moved behind the cameras, which were at the end of the room opposite the bandstand. An assistant collected the soda cans from the musicians, who took their places and picked up their instruments. Several couples took their places on the dance floor.

"Background!" and Sharah, along with the others sitting at the table, immediately began looking with fake interest at the stage.

"Go!" A recording of a 1940s song began, while the musicians mimed playing and the dancers danced. Two backgrounders crossed in front of Sharah's table, pretending to talk. George took out a cigarette, put it in his mouth, lit it with a lighter that had been sitting near him on the table, took it from his mouth, blew out smoke, and then waved the cigarette in an intricate pattern that looked like a sideways figure eight.

The music was suddenly cut off, all except for a low, steady, nearly inaudible background beat that allowed the dialogue to be recorded while the dancers on the floor stayed in step. A tall, classically handsome actor in a khaki uniform walked over to the table where the actress playing Rosie was sitting. "Excuse me," he said in a strong Russian accent, clearly audible above the beat. "Would you care to dance?"

"I shouldn't," "Rosie" said. "I – I have a young man."

"I don't know how you do it in this country," the actor said, smiling. "But in my country, it is considered patriotic to keep soldiers on leave from feeling lonely. Even if it's only one dance."

Next to Sharah, George was still waving his cigarette to the beat. He did it two more times, then returned it to his mouth.

"Rosie" smiled and gave the Russian soldier her hand. He pulled her up and they began to dance. The music started again.

"Okay, stop!" Rosie and the Russian soldier smiled at each other and separated. Along with the other background actors, Sharah and George relaxed; those who had moved during the scene returned to their places.

The director conferred with the assistants for a moment, then walked over to where Rosie and the Russian soldier stood on the dance floor and talked with them in a low voice. "Okay, background people," one of the assistant directors yelled, "please do NOT look at the actors during the dialogue. You're enjoying the music and watching the dancers or the band. And please only pretend to talk to each other; no real sounds, please."

The director walked Rosie back to her table, then waved over the cameraman. "I want to try another angle," he said. "Angle it from Rosie's right; I want to pick up some of the people in background."

For a moment, just a moment, he looked up and seemed to look directly at Sharah – no, she thought, he was looking at George, who was fiddling with the fake cigarette.

"I want to give the impression of a busy, popular nightclub," he said to the young male assistant director, who was hovering nearby. "Keep that guy playing with the cigarette. And I want a bit more action behind them." He started talking to the cameraman again.

"Okay," said the assistant director, and ran over to the waiters. "When he starts doing the cigarette thing," he said, "I want you," he pointed at a waiter, "to pick up a water pitcher and pretend to fill glasses. And you," he pointed to a man at the next table, "when he starts to do that, stand up and walk towards the back."

"You like my moves?" George asked Sharah.

"It's a bit elaborate," Sharah admitted. "Do you do the same thing each time?"

"Yep," he said. "I find that doing something interesting keeps me alert, especially when I'm on camera. Directors like that. Smithson especially likes it. In fact, just between you and me, he taught me this specific move a while ago, and asked me to use it the next time an assistant asked me to play with a cigarette. You want me to teach it to you? Just in case."

"Just in case of what?" she asked.

He shrugged. "It's up to you," he said. "I'll understand if you don't want to."

"No, it's okay," she said. "It looks like it's going to take them a while to set up the cameras. Teach it to me."

She pulled a cigarette out of the pack and for the next few minutes, she practiced the moves that George had made with the cigarette. "Do you always use the same one?" she asked.

"No," he said. "The director, or one of his assistants, usually teaches it

27

to me. This one, however, is a bit special." He smiled. "I notice that you're not asking me how it's special, or why I'm doing it."

"Or who will understand it. Should I ask?" Sharah asked, keeping her tone calm, ordinary.

George hesitated. "No," he said. "Better if you don't. For now."

At that moment, Smithson yelled. "Okay, are we ready? Let's go."

"All right, we're trying the rehearsal again!" yelled the assistant. "Quiet on the set!" Sharah took a breath.

"Look up at me, honey!" One of the makeup people took out a paintbrush, and quickly touched up Sharah's lips. She then took out a comb and pushed back a stray lock of Sharah's hair. "I saw you playing with the cigarette," she said.

"I taught her my moves," said George.

"Good idea – just in case they want a woman to do it instead. I'll let the director know."

She ran up to the assistant director and whispered to him for a moment; he nodded. She then joined the rest of the crew as they left the set.

"Background!" The people at the tables turned their attention to the bandstand. The music started to play. The couples danced. Two people passed in front of Sharah's table. George lit his cigarette. The music cut off, the beat began, and the Russian soldier walked to Rosie's table. This time, the cameraman, guided carefully by an assistant, walked the camera over, following the actor playing the soldier, and then shifted until he was facing both actors – and, beyond them, the table where George and Sharah sat.

The stout young woman ran up and tapped the director on the shoulder. "Hold it!" the director yelled. The actor playing the Russian grimaced and went back to his place, while "Rosie" shook her head in disgust. The woman whispered in the director's ear.

"Shit," the director said, loud enough for everyone to hear. "With all these interruptions, do they really think this is going to even make it to edit? Okay, hurry up."

He began talking to the cameraman, while the woman strode to Sharah's table. "You George Wexler?" she asked.

George looked up at her and nodded.

"Sorry," she said. "But I need to pull you from the production. There are some people downstairs who want to talk to you."

Sharah watched George carefully. His face didn't change, except for a slight twitch at the corner of his eye. "Really?" he said. "Is it a family emergency? Otherwise, I don't see why I can't wait until the scene is

28

over."

The young woman shook her head. She was trying to look calm, competent, but her face was flushed and Sharah could see her hands were trembling slightly. "Sorry, but they really want to talk to you and they said it couldn't wait."

George nodded. He turned to Sharah and offered her the herbal cigarette. "Here," he said. "Your turn."

She stared at the cigarette. "Just do it exactly way I did it," he said, and smiled at the assistant director. "She's relatively new at this," he said. "I've been training her so that if she's ever actually given real business to do, or even a line, she won't be nervous."

"Of course," said the young woman. "But we need to go. They're holding up the shot for us."

"Right." George turned back to her and took a breath. "Go ahead," he said. "Don't be afraid to be on camera. And thank you." He smiled at Sharah and offered her the cigarette again. This time, she took it.

"Remember, light it with flair," he said. He nodded at the assistant director and stood up.

"What the hell is going on?" the director asked and came over, looking very angry. "Do I need to do everyone's job here? If he's needed downstairs, get him downstairs and get somebody else to do his shtick. Or can't you handle that?"

"She said she'd do it," said the assistant director, pointing at Sharah, who nodded.

"Then what's the problem?" asked the director crossly. "All she has to do is what he did in rehearsal. It doesn't take a genius. Now get him off the set."

The assistant director nodded energetically and walked toward the doors. Without another word, George followed and they both disappeared behind the black curtains in back.

"You," said a voice, and Sharah turned to see Smithson looked directly at her. She flushed. "You need another rehearsal?" he asked, his voice suddenly softer, less angry.

"No," she said with confidence. "I know what to do."

"Good," he said. "Okay, let's do this." He turned and shouted. "Lock down the set!"

Once again, all the makeup and costume people hustled out the door, while the actors checked their costumes and took their places. "Set locked!" called an assistant.

"Okay, this is a take," yelled the director. "Background!"

Sharah picked up the lighter that had been placed on the table, lit the cigarette, and put it in her mouth. She sucked on it until the tip began to glow, being careful not to inhale – while the cigarette was fake, she didn't need to start coughing at the beginning of a take.

"Go!" yelled the director.

The band mimed playing. The recorded music started. The couple crossed in front of her. The music stopped, and the thumping sound began. Couples danced. The soldier walked toward Rosie's table and the cameraman found his spot. "Excuse me," said the soldier, "would you care to dance?"

Absolutely, Sharah thought. She removed the cigarette, held it between her fore and middle fingers, smiled and looked beyond the cameraman at the musicians. Then, trying to look careless and happy, she moved her hand with the lit cigarette in the pattern that George taught her, staying with the beat of the music.

The Russian soldier held out his hand and Rosie took it. They went to the dance floor, the camera following, and began to dance. The music started up again.

"Cut!" the director yelled. "That's a take! Okay, we're running late, let's take a 10-minute break and then set up for the next shot."

"Break!" yelled the assistant directors. The tall young man came over to Sharah's side of the room. "Ten minutes, folks," he said loudly. "We'll let you know when we want you back."

Sharah slipped off her high heels, picked them up in one hand, took her clutch in the other, and stood. The assistant director walked over to her. "Nice work!" he said to one of the waiters walking past. "And you too," he said quietly. "The director wanted me to tell you that he appreciated the way you stepped in at the last moment."

"No problem," Sharah said. "And if it's appropriate, you can let him know that I'm available for any other specific background work that may be necessary."

"Good to know," the assistant said. He smiled briefly, and then ran back to the director.

Sharah pushed through the two black curtains that protected the set, heading back to holding. She didn't want to think about what had happened – was happening – to George. She had no idea what message she had sent with her cigarette or who would receive it when the episode aired in two days' time. And she would need to have a talk with her mother when she got home and make plans – just in case.

With that came a moment of pure panic. She hurriedly strode into the ladies' room, went into one of the stalls, leaned against the door, and took several deep breaths.

Once her heart stopped racing and the fear passed, Sharah realized that she actually felt pretty damn good – better than she had for a long time. She had done something. The message would be sent. She was now part of something important, something that might eventually stop the political steamroller that was threatening her and her family.

It was only a very small part – Sharah was, after all, a backgrounder, figuratively and literally. She had no lines to say and nobody outside of the set would know her name or what she did. Their eyes, and the eyes of future historians, would be on the main actors. But without her – and all the other anonymous people she worked with – it wouldn't get done.

"Anyone in here?" a woman called from the door of the bathroom. "They're calling us back on set."

Sharah opened the door. "Already?" she asked. The woman grimaced.

"Do you believe it? That's some ten minutes. Either they completely ignore us or they can't do without us."

Sharah grinned at her. "I guess," she said, "the show must go on."

THE SEVENTH STREET MATRIARCHY
MARIE VIBBERT

I was stuck at the traffic light at Seventh Street and Red Avenue when a young white man came out of nowhere. He slammed his palm on my passenger door window and shouted, "Get out of the car!"

I don't know if he had a gun or if I just imagined he did, but I popped my seatbelt, opened my door, and took off running, five-inch heels, pencil skirt and all. I wish my high school track coach could have seen that sprint.

There's nothing at the intersection of Seventh and Red except three churches and the Riverview Estates public housing development. I didn't stop to pick a direction, so I ended up with the Episcopalians.

I tell you, ten years as a public housing worker in a big city like Cleveland, and it's my first day out in a small town that I get carjacked.

There was another woman already behind the flying buttress of the Episcopal Church, one of those older white women so transparent they seem to be made of netting. She had a wide canvas shoulder bag she was holding in front of herself like a shield.

Together we peeked around the stone column to see the boy crawling behind my steering wheel and staring at it like he'd never seen one. Why, he was just a baby! He couldn't be a year over thirteen.

"That boy is not from here," the white woman said.

I checked that 911 got my text. "You don't know that," I said.

"I mean," the old woman said, leaning over her bag for emphasis, "he isn't from our project."

She said it like pro-check. "You stay at Riverview Estates?" I asked, with new solicitousness. "Have you met your case worker?"

"Case workers! Bah!" she said. She kept her eyes on the action. The white boy fumbled with the car controls and it shuddered and stalled. He spun in the seat, panicked.

"Well, my name is Ty'Shae Walker, and I've been assigned to Riverview Estates by the county housing–"

She cut me off. "Bea is going to hear about this!"

The police finally pulled up with a siren-burp. The young man looked relieved, his eyes closed, resting as the police pulled him out. Something about that, about his posture, tickled my instincts. It wasn't right.

What with my car in the middle of it all, there was nothing to do but wait. I wished I could close my door, though. The battery wasn't the newest.

The officer who took my statement was a good four inches shorter than me, and I could tell he was trying very hard not to look at my chest. "Did you see anyone chasing the boy, ma'am?"

"No, sir, I wish I had had the calm at the time to notice more details, but I simply ran. Does that boy have a record?"

"I'm sure I don't know, ma'am."

I fished around in my purse for my phone and my business cards. "Well I'm a case worker for the housing department, and…"

"He's not FROM HERE," the old woman repeated, still holding her bag in front of her like a shield.

***

Riverview Estates had no view of the river, but mature oak trees shaded the sides of the building and there was that odd urban-yet-rural feel you get in small cities. I could see the blank wall of a pre-fab warehouse through the trees and a row of green beans staked out along the chain-link fence.

A little girl stood on the steps leading up to one of the housing project's entrances. Her fists were balled on her hips and her face was as tightly drawn as her little blond pigtails. "You gotta do what I say, Ant'ny. Momma left *me* in charge."

Ant'ny was on the ground in front of the steps, still taller than her, his sunburned scalp shining right through his blonde buzz cut as he ducked his head.

Wasn't that familiar! My last day at Outhwaite Homes I saw a little girl in adorable puffs, shaking her finger upward at her lanky brother. I loved the fierce little Amazons as much as I feared their power rose from sexism. Since its inception, public housing rules favor families with children and retirees with disabilities. These groups are largely female, and it forces a de facto matriarchy, but one with the same prejudices we all have, that girls "mature faster" and have to be better behaved, while "boys will be boys."

I closed my car door and they both turned to gape at me. "Hello children," I said. "Is this building C?"

Ant'ny nodded, but the girl scowled. "We don't talk to no strangers!"

"I'm not a stranger. I'm a social worker. My name is Ms. Walker. Is your mother home?"

The girl folded her arms. "No. Momma had to work. That's why I'm in charge!"

"She left you children all alone? What's your last name?"

"We aren't supposed to answer personal questions, either." The girl lost some of her bluster. "Anyway, Auntie Bea is watching us from the window. That's why I was telling Ant'ny we can't go past the bushes. He wanted to run all the way to the end of the building!"

"Momma said 'in sight.' That's in sight."

"I think I'll talk to Auntie Bea, then," I said.

The little girl spread her arms, blocking my path. "Maybe Aunt Bea doesn't want to talk to no government people!"

"That's enough, Flora." An older white woman opened the door. "I'll talk to you, miss. I'm Bea Jacobs."

"Ty'Shae Walker," I said, holding out my hand. "From Housing."

The woman didn't take my hand, but she looked at it like she might. "We haven't had a visit from the housing authority in a long time. We handle most things on our own here at Riverview." She was one of those plump, vigorous mature women, solid as stone and wrapped in layers of thrift store brocade like castle walls.

"I appreciate that, I do, but I'm new to your community and I have some questions. I just know a local lady can help me best." I gave her my most winning smile. "You know, I grew up in public housing, myself."

Bea did not look like that particularly recommended me to her, but she grudgingly led me to her apartment. It was very tidy and pleasant. She left me to settle on the sofa and put a kettle on the stove. "So are you trying to evict us?" she asked.

"Heavens, no! Did you know you are one of the last public housing developments in the country? I'd sooner smash a Tiffany window." I secretly suspected this was because the population of the residence was, like the surrounding community, 89% white, but I kept that to myself. I was grateful enough there was one still standing.

Bea crossed her arms, a stolid wall between me and the kitchen. "Red Rose or Cinnamon Stick?"

"Black tea is fine. Anyway, I was confused about a few things. Just getting my bearings as your new caseworker. I'm perplexed how few men are in the residence. It's improbably below expectation, and there's a very eligible young man with two little boys…"

"I don't control who gets in. That's your department." The kettle whistled and she went to attend to it.

Well, of course it was my department, or rather the local housing authority I worked for. But it just didn't make sense. The county had a long line of perfectly acceptable candidates who had been refused, all of them male or married couples with a male member, and the housing rules rewarded married couples with children like they were made of pure funding. I'd hoped a local resident might provide context I was missing, something only someone living here might notice.

Bea set a mug in front of me. My father drank Red Rose tea. The smell was comforting. She turned the handle toward me almost exactly the way he would. She sat down with the long, slow sigh of age. "Men are more likely to commit crimes," she said, "and crime disqualifies. I think you'll find that's the reason. We have a good, law-abiding community here."

"I like to be a part of the community I serve. I want you to know you can talk to me if you have problems."

"We don't have problems."

She said it a little too fast and firmly. This fine upstanding woman was hiding something from me.

***

The boy who had attempted to steal my car was one Martin Navarre, fourteen years old. He lived not two blocks from the development with his uncle and two cousins. Public housing would have provided his parents with the stability to keep Martin, I could see that in the case records. Instead they were both working agricultural jobs where they weren't allowed to have family with them. I found their repeated applications to Riverview and no explanation in our system as to why they were turned down, why poor Martin had been left in a situation so awful he tried to steal a car to get out of it.

The truly peculiar thing was how none of the records in the database were associated with a username. It almost looked like the database had edited itself. Well, there was one person who had to have signed off on these decisions: my boss.

Mike Kolowski and I did not hit it off. Like many of my past supervisors, he was not a social worker by choice. I got the impression he was tricked into it on his way to a political career. He wore sports t-shirts under a tan suit jacket. Through the course of my orientation, he told me I thought I was better than him since I came from Cleveland, that the Irish were the real slaves, and no one had ever helped him in any way. Oh, and "Women in public housing deserve their situation because they couldn't hold on to their men."

Mr. Kolowski was everything my papa warned me would be waiting for me if I moved to a small town. I just hadn't expected to find it all in one body.

In answer to my question about the inconsistencies in the application records, he said, "Leave it. I just got word–"

"But sir, it looks like you haven't logged in for a while, and it should be your account that approves final disposition of requests." There were no log-ins recorded for him ever, actually, but I was being polite.

"I sign everything," he said curtly. "On paper, and my assistant puts it in the system."

"Could I see the paper copies?"

"Do I look like a secretary? Anyway, we're shutting down Riverview at last. Your new assignment is to relocate the residents."

I straightened my spine. "I beg your pardon?"

"The land is sold. We're getting out of the brick and mortar business. Every city is. We have to do what everyone else is doing."

"Because it's right or because it's convenient?"

"What's right is what's convenient," he said. He shifted a pile of papers that was slowly falling over. I'd never seen so many pieces of paper in my life. I picked up some that had fallen to the floor. They were emails. Printed emails.

I shuddered for the planet. "You can get these on your phone now," I said, trying for helpful as I set the papers on top of the stack. "You know, I suspect the relocation program itself will cost as much as keeping Riverview open another four years. It's been safely in the black for every fiscal since–"

He scowled and flapped his hand at me like a handkerchief. "Why does a woman your height wear heels? It's like talking to a giraffe."

"Sir, I want to look out for the best interests of our residents."

"Look out for yourself, sweetheart. It's the only way to get ahead."

In a firmer voice, I asked, "Who would have the authority to cancel the sale?"

Mr. Kolowski's face got deep red and he rose out of his seat. "That housing project is a blight on this community and it is my intention to kill it as quickly as possible. Relocate the people or don't. I don't really care. They can stay where they are while the wrecking balls hit the walls."

***

Bea Jacobs folded her arms and didn't move from her doorway.

I said, "I'm afraid I have some rather sensitive issues to discuss with all of the residents. May I come in?"

She said nothing. It was unfair. I didn't want to be there any more than she wanted me there, with the news I had. I tried a different tactic. "Ms. Jacobs, I have some good news." It helps to frame change in as positive a light as possible. "The housing department is going to help you find your own place, a real house."

"I have no intention of leaving," she said. It sounded like she meant the doorway as well as the apartment.

"I know you would rather stay, but think of this as an opportunity. We'll find you a place with modern conveniences and no stairs to walk up. And you'll be closer to social services."

"Why would I want to live all on my own? My neighbors are like family. We look out for each other."

She was only the first of one hundred and twenty residents I had to speak with. There was no time to keep beating around the bush. "The city is shutting down Riverview. We have to relocate everyone before the building is torn down."

"That's not going to happen." She said it with perfect authority, like it was her decision.

"I'm afraid it's already happening, Ms. Jacobs. The city has sold the property to a developer. There's no more funding for housing of this kind. We can get you into a private home on a rent subsidy."

She smirked and put one hand on the door behind her. "I'm sorry you came all this way, and I appreciate the warning, but you have to leave, now."

"Ms. Jacobs, getting rid of me won't solve anything. I'm here to help you."

But she'd closed the door before I finished speaking.

Little Ant'ny had wandered into the hallway and squinted up at me. "You're tall," he said.

"Thank you," I said. "Do you know any other adults who are home right now?"

He wiped his nose on the back of his hand, squinted sagely, and asked, "What's in it for me?"

***

For a handful of candy, little Ant'ny took me around, but it was to no avail. No one wanted to move. Doors were slammed in my face, no doubt in fear of being served eviction papers. I was beginning to wish I had eviction papers drawn up.

I had done a lot of work! Four options, minimum, for each resident. Background checks on landlords. Relocation assistance. Bus routes and mixed income communities – all those subtle factors to find a niche, a comfortable home. Nope. No, thank you, we're quite happy here.

I stood next to my car in the fading afternoon, wilting like a sunflower, and said, "Please, Lord, do not make me have to talk to my supervisor."

***

"Just keep going back," Mr. Kolowski said, never looking up from the baseball game he was watching on his tablet. "Print eviction notices, slide it under their doors. Bam. Done."

"We can't evict without cause–"

"Actually, we can." He snapped his fingers, looking at me for the first time. "Better yet, threaten them. Yeah, no paperwork needed for that. Nothing legally binding. Like – hint that the relocation deal could go away and they'd be homeless."

Well, what can you say to that? I turned on my heel and directed my questions to the computer system, which, really, has always been my most cooperative coworker.

I didn't want to, but first I looked for grounds for evictions. I didn't find any. Not so much as a noise complaint. The local police hardly patrolled Riverview because the rate of incidents was the lowest of any block in the city. I mean, how about that? No late rent payments. Not a single drug possession. They had a youth choir and a softball team. The more I looked in to it, the more I saw Riverview was just about a perfect implementation of low-income housing. I jotted down some notes for a possible article on the subject, but I had nothing to solve my problem of how to compassionately evict an entire, happy community.

"Ms. Walker?" A pale, waifish girl with colorless hair poked my shoulder. "I'm Emily, Mr. Kolowski's assistant? Can I use the computer, please?"

I counted it a stroke of luck. "Emily, I am delighted to make your acquaintance." I took her hand in both of mine. "Can you show me where you file Mr. Kolowski's papers?"

I found the Navarre family applications. All three, all stamped with a green rubber stamp that read "Approved" and bore Mr. Kolowski's signature.

I went back to the computer and tapped Emily's shoulder. "Can you just show me how you input these decisions in the system?"

She finished the job she was doing while I watched, and then did another. Emily's methods were perfectly orthodox. "Go back and look at the past twenty applications? There – you see – here is the one you just input, and it says your name and the result – but look at this one – who input that?"

Emily frowned. "But that's..." she opened the record. "I don't get it. I put this one in, myself. I remember it, and it was 'approved' not 'denied.' And... look see the change log..." She got the panicked look of someone in fear for their job. "I swear I entered this. There should be a log but there isn't. I... you have to believe me! Someone else undid my work! And they deleted the change log."

"I believe you," I assured her. "Someone else is changing things, and I think I know who it is, too."

***

Bea met me at the sidewalk, a bulwark in a white blazer, pacing back and forth like a sentry. Her calves were like cannon balls over her patent leather flats.

"Thank you for seeing me on such short notice," I said.

She came to a smart parade rest. "I'm not leaving."

"Of course you're not! I wouldn't dream of making you! This is more in the line of how I can help you stay," I said. I saw the shift in her posture and face. Then I gently laid down my accusation. "I know about the meddling in the housing database. I suspect you do, too."

"I'm a retired veteran of the armed forces. I don't need to–"

"Ma'am? I wasn't alone when I figured it out. Stalling will only give that other person more time to wonder what I'm doing about it and maybe start doing things themselves. Help me help you."

Bea's eyes bulged. Her cheeks twitched. "Fine." She turned on one foot and marched into the grass. She led me around the building to a maintenance door, and pulled a key ring from her belt.

"Should you have the key to this?" I asked.

She yanked the metal door open and gestured for me to go in first. I momentarily feared she meant to lock me in a closet, but there was nothing menacing in her stance. In fact, she looked embarrassed, so I went in.

The narrow room twinkled with a thousand little lights that swayed as I entered. It was warm, too, and gently breezy. For a second I felt like I'd stepped through some fairy gate into another world.

Then Bea switched on the light.

Phones hung from power cords like flat square grapes on bundled vines, tied up and down at different heights, their cords looped and twist-tied. Their different sizes and colors made it a ragged arrangement.

The floor was clean under my heels. Someone had bolted an aluminum ladder to the wall. That was what the phones hung from. I turned to look at Bea. "There is no way this was allowed by your renter's agreement."

She tilted her head as if to say that was a fair guess. "It took us ten years to build this cluster. Ten years and everyone pitching in."

"Ms. Jacobs? I should report this. This…" I failed to find a word for it.

"Data processing cluster. I wiped the original operating systems and installed my own. I was a systems programmer, supported my family well, until my Derek got cancer. They canned me the next day to get us off the insurance." She reached up, cupping a knock-off iPhone lovingly. "But I still remember my trade. I call it my cybernetic social worker."

You know that made me feel some kinda way. "I appreciate that you've done a lot, but you knew this was a rental unit and if need be, you'd have to leave it behind."

She waved her hand dismissively. "My cluster has shot down plans to close Riverview a half-dozen times."

"Yes, but it's not working this time, is it? And I know why."

I could see her anger, and that she knew I was right. Her great proud shoulders sagged and she looked almost frail. "I don't understand it," she said, eyes scanning helplessly over the silent phone screens. "There's nothing on any of the servers, no contracts, nothing."

"Yes," I said. "And I know why. Would you like my help, Ms. Jacobs?"

Bea avoided looking at me by re-arranging some cables that looked particularly kinked. "Look at these phones. We got most of them from the gutter. Not even in the garbage. They weren't worth walking to the can."

"Let me help you, and nothing will be left in the gutter."

"So *help me*! What's stopping you?"

It was my turn to fold my arms. "I couldn't abide helping you if you don't start letting men into the project."

"Oh come on!" she said, like I was withholding in the name of repainting the cabinets.

"I'm serious. You help me, and some deserving young men, and I help you. Otherwise it's no deal. I'll continue doing my job, and that includes reporting this unauthorized… home improvement."

Bea chewed her lip for a minute. She returned to the door. "Let's actually have that cup of tea."

***

The cluster was a virtual lawyer and bureaucrat – it searched quickly through precedents and procedures and produced the best possible outcomes. According to it, Riverview Estates should have been free to operate in perpetuity.

Except someone was working outside of the system, offline, offbook.

I would stake my life on whom: Mike Kolowski made an intern print his emails for him.

"Yes, it sounds like him. Mike Kolowski wanted to sell this land five years ago," Bea said, and paused as she refilled the teakettle at the sink. She bent over the stove and blew at the burner to help it light. "I put the kibosh on that by filing for historic status for our 1930s streamline architecture." She leaned against the kitchen archway and pointed at the window. "Didja notice the darker brick lines on the outside of the building? They make this box pattern around the windows. Classic WPA style. Anyway, it's true even if the state government overturned the ruling. Corporate shills."

"Ms. Jacobs? I know where he keeps his paper records. I could photograph and email you what I find. It could cost me my job or get me arrested. I'm willing to do it, if you stop blocking men from moving in."

"It wouldn't be Riverview anymore! They'd be fighting and working on cars and…"

So help me if she said "barbecuing" next I would lose my ladylike demeanor. "I told you I was raised in the projects, Ms. Jacobs, but I didn't say by whom."

"So you had a good dad, so what?"

I had the best dad, actually, and he raised my sisters and me all on his own, but I could tell she wasn't prepared to hear it. "It's my final offer. You know there's no time to waste."

She snatched a towel from a hippo-shaped hook and started wiping the counter like she was murdering the stains. "You do everything right. You follow all the rules. And look what it gets you."

"Ms. Jacobs? You really didn't follow ALL the rules."

Her vigorous scrubbing slowed a touch. "You know what I mean," she said.

***

Mr. Kolowski had a habit of coming in early and staying late, for all that he seemed to spend most of his time watching sports or talking on the phone to his wife, daughter, and various contractors about his new garage door installation.

I learned more about him than I'd like while I hung around, combing his filing cabinets. The Riverview sale information wasn't there.

At last he got up and put his coat on. "You going to sort shit all night?"

"Oh, no, I'm all done here," I said, closing the drawer. "I'll see you tomorrow."

I hid in the ladies'. I felt like a teenager, peering through the door-crack until I saw his office light turn off.

His desk drawer had a manila folder labeled "Riverview Condos." Bingo. There was a letter from a developer and receipts for substantial sums, made out to Mr. Kolowski himself and deposited in a private bank. Why, he wasn't even doing this honestly! I started taking photos with my phone.

The door opened, flooding me with hallway light. Mr. Kolowski froze, reaching for a lunch box left on a chair by the door. I froze too, and we stared at each other a long second before he said, "Hey! What do you think you're doing?"

I straightened and closed the folder neatly. "Calling your boss, Mr. Kolowski."

"About what? Hey! I'm your boss! You are fired!"

I walked right up to him and don't you know he about collapsed to make room for me? Not so brave now we were both standing. I looked down at him. "You start your paperwork, sir, and I'll start mine. Have a blessed day."

***

Flora and Ant'ny chased each other around and through the leaf pile, scattering it all over the lawn of Riverview Building C. Flora bossed Ant'ny through picking up handfuls of leaves to re-build the piles in adorable, childish inefficiency. Their mother sat on the bottom step, snapping peas.

Martin Navarre, newly moved with his mother and father into Apartment 202-B, was washing their front window and smiling proudly at his work. Bea sighed contentedly next to me on the top step. Martin had done more to change her mind about boys than I had by being the most solicitous and eager young helper around the grounds. He'd make up chores for himself if he didn't have enough. He was that happy not to be with his uncle anymore.

I admired my new business card. Head of Housing Services. "You didn't have anything to do with my promotion, did you?"

She made a smug sound that could be denied but was almost certainly a yes.

"Does this mean I'm in your matriarchy now? Don't go making me mayor or anything. I can keep Riverview open just fine where I am."

Bea's soft, full arm brushed mine. "You're thinking small, Ty'Shae."

She handed me her phone, which had information on a state funding issue. "I figure we start with Ohio, then expand nationally."

"You know, I think you're right." Columbus had a perfect site for a new housing development, and it was on a river, too.

WE SPEAK IN TONGUES OF FLAME
J L GEORGE

This town doesn't look like it belongs here. That's why Keris likes it.

Its pale buildings, in their stubborn regularity, don't fit the valley walls, but the builders wedged them along its sides anyway. The landscape looks liable to buck and writhe at any moment, scattering the houses like flies, revealing the oozing little sores where they have dug themselves in.

Inflexibility is this nation's watchword. The road along the valley floor runs perfectly straight; deviates for no hillock or stream or ancestral farmstead. Soldiers in blue and white march along it at midday, salute the town hall in the neat white square where Keris plies her trade, then turn and resume their marching.

She makes a game of it, sometimes, trying to break their concentration. She has chalks in all the bright colours of the insect kingdom, and when she starts early, she can cover a quarter of the square in flowers and monsters and women with flowing tresses before they arrive. A young recruit forgot himself and stared, once, and the blush that coloured his face when she caught him looking warmed her from within for days.

It wasn't a warmth born of lust, or even, really, of pride. It was pure, clean spite.

Keris covers the blank white stones with beauty, and the townsfolk smile and drop coins into her hat, and, hating them, she smiles back. She speaks only to a select few, though she knows their language well enough. Her voice always betrays her, her accent never quite hidden. They start to look at her with pity; speak to her more slowly; tell her how very talented she is, considering.

Today, the soldiers come late, marching prisoners along with them.

One of the prisoners raises her eyes, not yet quite worn down by the grinding trek inland. She's dirty, her trousers ragged, and she walks with a limp, but her eyes widen at the sight of Keris and her pictures.

The sentence is read out, the prisoners dragged away to await its completion. As she stumbles after the soldiers, the woman spits out a curse in the old tongue.

44

It has been so long since Keris has heard it. She stares open-mouthed after the woman, and cannot tear her eyes away until the prisoners are long gone. Not that she could have spoken a reply aloud, unless she wanted to follow them.

That night it rains hard, washing the square clean of the traces of her old pictures. In the morning, Keris draws flames.

***

The men in blue and white came with fire. Keris didn't know their tongue back then; she could not understand what they shouted, and heard only the baying of beasts. The smoke hurt her eyes and her throat; she could not see; she clung so hard to her mother's hands that it hurt them both.

The men still prised them apart. They rifled through her mother's papers, and what they found they held aloft, snarling and pointing to the words as though to say, *You see?*

Keris hadn't understood. Every child had to learn to read and write. How could it be a sin?

When she first came to this town, she wrote poetry on the flagstones. The people sniffed and turned up their noses. She hadn't learned their language perfectly then, and they did not understand hers. They liked her better when she started drawing pictures. Now, seeing smoke and flame in place of birds and butterflies, they start to turn up their noses again.

That evening, sitting alone in the square after the people have dispersed, Keris draws the prisoner from the market square. Black for her long straight hair, auroral green for her eyes, and quick thumb-smudged lines for her endless movement, for how she refused to give up her struggle.

The work is messier than usual, and less beautiful, but Keris sits and looks at it for a long time after she finishes. At times, she has to stop herself from speaking to it as though it were alive.

***

In the morning, the picture has faded. Keris finds herself unable to settle to drawing anything else until she completes it again, and all day, she feels the prisoner's eyes on her as she works.

The real prisoner, the woman from the square, is probably gone by now. Dragged to the capital for execution, or to the mines for hard labour. That's what happens when you fight. But her portrait keeps Keris

45

company, a steady presence at her side.

She works unmolested through the day, the occasional coin landing in her hat, though for the most part the townspeople pass her by. When she bundles up her chalks to leave, though, she realises there is something subtly different about the portrait. Some of the movement is gone from it. The tilt of its head is not so pronounced. If it were a real person, Keris would think that it had stopped all of a sudden, catching sight of her.

Somebody must have walked over it; smudged it with their feet. Still, Keris doesn't correct it before she goes, and she doesn't rub out the picture.

***

She draws the prisoner most days, now. Sometimes she switches the colours, gives her hair of forest green or plummy red. Eyes of honey-gold. Sometimes she draws the prisoner standing still and tall, or sitting cross-legged, or smiling. There's nothing she can do for the woman from the square, but she can give peace to her in pictures.

Keris draws enough animals and flowers and flowing-haired mermaids to garner her a few coins, though at the end of the day, her hat is no longer so heavy as it once was. The rest of the time, she draws flames. Sometimes, she imagines that the prisoner smiles to see them.

She no longer stops herself from talking to the picture. One afternoon, singing under her breath as she works, she's startled to find that it's a lullaby in the old language, one that her mother used to sing. She hadn't realised she remembered it.

***

Little by little, Keris withdraws.

At the tavern where she takes supper, she contents herself with thin soup and bread—lucky, really, since her hat is growing lighter by the day—and replies in monosyllables to the few townsfolk who greet her. In the square, she avoids eye-contact with passers-by, and, increasingly, they avoid looking at her. Yet she is not lonely. Sometimes she's sure she feels somebody standing behind her, watching her as she draws, but when she glances over her shoulder she sees only the prisoner, returning her regard with flat, steady eyes.

A column of soldiers passes through with more captives. They don't overnight in the town this time, and these prisoners are skinnier, more ragged. These prisoners do not fight. When Keris forgets herself and cries out in the old tongue, none answer. Only one—an old man, his beard thinning, his shirt hanging off the knobs of his bony shoulders—catches her eye, and when he does, he gives a warning shake of his head.

She sleeps badly that night, and wakes early. After a half-hour's shifting and fidgeting in her bed, she gives up and gathers her chalks.

Light is just beginning to brush the edges of the sky when she arrives in the square, the outlines of the hills coming slowly into relief. Mist hangs in their hollows; hovers above the road. For a moment, Keris thinks that *she* is a figment of the mist, too—a woman with long straight hair and ragged trousers, standing in the spot where Keris usually sits on the ground among her drawings.

But there is no mist in the town square, and as Keris moves closer, the woman remains. Her back is turned, and she crouches and lays her palm against the flagstones.

"Hello?" Keris calls, in the local tongue. The woman makes no move to acknowledge her. Keris hesitates a moment, worrying at her lower lip, before she speaks again. "Are you looking for me?" she asks falteringly in the old tongue, and the woman stands and turns toward her.

Even in the morning half-light, the face is unmistakable. Keris has drawn it often enough. The prisoner smiles at her and holds out a hand.

Then vanishes as the sun creeps above the hills.

Keris does not realise she has cried out until she hears the sound echo back from the walls of the square; does not realise she has sunk to her knees until she feels the hard flagstones beneath them. Something cold has wedged itself behind her ribs, and it makes her gasp.

***

She cannot get rid of the cold. It dulls to a nagging ache as the day wears on, but it's always there. Soup doesn't warm her, and neither does her mother's woollen shawl around her shoulders. All night Keris shivers beneath her bedcovers, and in the morning she's awake before the dawn once more, creeping to the square in the grey.

The prisoner is there, in the same spot where Keris drew her portrait yesterday. Again, she turns and holds out her hand when Keris calls to her in the old tongue. Again, she vanishes with the rising of the sun.

Again, a cold splinter lodges itself behind Keris's ribs, and she shivers with it until the sun is high over the town.

It is the same the next day. And the next.

***

47

One evening, as Keris eats her soup before the open fire in the tavern, the landlady comes to sit at her table. She has always been friendly enough. She tried to teach Keris to lose her accent once, thinking that that might mean a few more silver coins in her hat, though eventually they both gave it up as a bad job. Now, she frowns and says, "Are you sick? You're not eating enough. And you're pale as ash."

The landlady reaches out as though she means to touch Keris's cheek, but then thinks better of it and tucks her hand into the crook of her elbow.

"I'm fine," Keris tells her.

"If you don't feel better soon," the landlady goes on, ignoring her, "you should go to see the wisewoman."

The wisewoman lives on the outskirts of town, further up the hillside than anybody else, and she speaks of gods that mean nothing to Keris. She did cure a bout of the sneezing sickness that had kept Keris in bed for a week, once; but Keris is fairly sure that had more to do with the herbs than with what the wisewoman chanted over them.

"I'll think about it," she says, tugs her shawl more tightly about her and turns back to her soup.

***

Keris knows she is not ill. But for the sliver of ice that makes its home in her chest each morning, she feels fine; good, even. She sleeps little but tires little; though her meals are scanty, sometimes she fizzes with energy so effervescent she feels that her heels will leave the ground. When she draws the prisoner, sometimes she is surprised to look up from her work and find herself still earthbound.

She no longer draws butterflies, or flowers, or mermaids with flowing tresses. She draws only the prisoner, and flames. At the end of each day, she still finds a few coins in her hat—but the townspeople who put them there do so with expressions of pity and not of admiration.

Keris would like to throw the money back in their faces. Only the fear that she will be dragged away, her chalks taken, keeps her from doing so.

These days, the town is thick with soldiers. They march through twice a day, sometimes more frequently, and those arriving from the west rarely come without prisoners. The townspeople mutter of insurrection, of dangerous anarchists hiding out in caves along the coast, and Keris thinks of her mother's books thrown on the pyre as the men in blue and white denounced her.

Then she draws more flames.

She is still cold. The prisoner remains a phantom; and, finally, she decides she needs somebody who deals in phantoms, and makes the trek up the hillside to the wisewoman's cottage.

No dank, weed-grown little hut, this. This town demands its buildings hold to the pattern, and so the wisewoman's home is of the same generous proportion and regular outline as the rest, built of the same pale stone. Only the statuette of a goddess at the entrance, the sweet curl of incense smoke from one of the wide windows, show the place for what it is.

The door opens before Keris can knock, and the wisewoman beckons her inside. She's of indeterminate age—certainly no crone, though the hair piled up on her head is shot through with grey —and she smiles and offers Keris sweet tea from the pot keeping warm above her fire. Keris did not mean to take anything from her, wary of what it might mean to do so, but the warmth of the tea and the crackle of the fire sing to the cold inside her. Sitting before the flames, her hands wrapped around the cup, she can almost imagine feeling warm again.

"You're looking for a ghost," the wisewoman tells her.

Keris shakes her head. "No," she says, then stops, frowning. After all, the woman she saw in the town square may well be dead by now. Perhaps it is her spirit that Keris sees each day in the haze of dawn. She sighs and looks down into her tea. "Maybe. I've been—drawing somebody. Every day. Sometimes I feel as if she's really there, watching over me. And in the morning I see her. I call out to her, but she never stays."

"Because you do not call her by name," the wisewoman says.

"I don't know her name."

"Have you asked?"

***

Keris had expected something more. Smoke and chanting, or the bones of one of the skinny mountain rabbits tossed into a cauldron, or at the very least an injunction to drink some bitter herbal concoction. (Back home, it would have been the bones.) She finds herself unconvinced, but the following morning, she stands once more in the town square and sees the prisoner before her, a spectre trembling before the dawn.

"Who are you?" she calls, and the prisoner smiles and vanishes.

She spends the day scowling to herself; drawing her flames with enough force that she breaks her yellow chalk.

It is only later that it occurs to her she called out in the local tongue. It's still a habit with her. Perhaps the prisoner does not understand it.

She has drawn only flames all day, but in the evening, as the square begins to empty, she draws the prisoner again with painstaking care. Each strand of her hair must look real enough to touch, and each crinkle at the corner of her eye bring her face to life. Keris sits back on her heels, satisfied, when she is done. She can almost imagine that the picture will answer her if she speaks to it.

***

The next morning, she calls out, "Wait!" in the old tongue, and the prisoner turns smiling to face her.

Keris is breathless. "Tell me your name?"

She's rusty in the old tongue, and she mutates where it isn't necessary, a tic that Grandmother used to say sounded common, and that got her knuckles rapped more than once as a child. If Mother was around, an argument would inevitably follow; but later Mother would still take her aside and explain that people would think her unschooled if she spoke that way.

The prisoner doesn't seem to notice. Her smile breaks like a wave into the sparkling shower of her laughter. "My name is Arlau," she says.

It takes Keris a moment to realise the name is a pun in the old tongue. *Ar lo*, by hand. She laughs out loud with the delight of recognition, and then sobers, shamed at her surprise. "No," she says, "your real name."

"Real enough," Arlau tells her, and takes her by the hand. Her skin is warm and dry as the grass-snakes Keris used to set loose in Grandmother's bedroom when she was small.

"You mean you'll stay?"

"Where else would I go?"

***

Arlau perches on the steps behind Keris's spot in the square and watches her draw. In person, her eyes are the colour of sunlight through green glass, and though she sits very still, there is an incipient sense of movement coiled up in her that Keris could never hope to capture with her chalks.

All day, Arlau's eyes follow her—or sometimes the birds that cross the sky above the square, or the skinny stray cats who scrounge for scraps of food, or the branches of the ornamental trees shifting in the breeze. She never looks at the faces of the passers-by, and they ignore her in return.

The coins they drop into Keris's hat are sporadic, now; but then, these days, she draws only flames.

Arlau traces them with her hands, bright spots of chalk on the pads of her fingers. "Have you ever thought," she asks, dreamily, "what else you might make real by drawing?"

Keris takes her hand and holds it tight, and tells her she mustn't talk like that. She'll be arrested, dragged away, and this time Keris will have no chalks and no words from the wisewoman to bring her back.

Arlau only shrugs and glances around the square with calm indifference. "They can't understand us," she points out.

The realisation startles Keris. She speaks the old tongue more and more often these days, her fluency returning, her accent making itself heard a little more stubbornly when she speaks with the locals. They don't understand her and Arlau, but they cast her curious sideways glances, and she is always careful to make herself small when the soldiers march through the square.

At night, Arlau shares her mattress in the room she rents. Her warm hands are skilful, and sometimes Keris forgets that she is not the prisoner from the square and asks if she has had women as lovers before. Arlau just laughs and says, "I have only you," and holds her closer.

Autumn is coming in, and the nights grow cold quickly once the sun is down. The bare hillsides hold few trees, and kindling is expensive. Keris lacks the money to keep her room heated until morning. They shiver and squirm to keep their hands and feet tucked under the covers, and finally, Arlau touches the side of her face and says, "Draw me a fire."

Keris does as she's bid, though she can see little point in it, in the dark. She crouches over the grate, the floor turning her bare feet to ice, and draws flames on the back wall. The task absorbs her; she finds that she is humming. It's the same song her mother used to sing, the one she once thought she had forgotten.

"My mother used to sing this," Arlau says, as though she has plucked the thought out of Keris's skull. "When I was very small."

"Mine too."

"I know."

It occurs to Keris to ask how, but then Arlau jumps to her feet and bounds over to join her at the fire. "What?" she asks, frowning a little to see Arlau grin so childishly.

Arlau nudges her with her shoulder. "Can't you feel it?"

Keris blinks at her, the firelight dancing softly on her face, the heat of the fire caressing both of them like a mother's touch. A small gasp breaks out of her. Then she falls back on her heels, and a shout of joyful laughter pulls itself from her lungs.

***

In the morning, Keris's landlady tells her she will have to leave. Keris is too noisy, she says: she keeps the other boarders up at night with her talking and laughing. The landlady refunds her the rest of the month's rent and refuses to look at Arlau.

Keris walks the streets with her hands shoved deep into the pockets of her old coat. The town is too regular, too sensibly laid out, and she cannot get lost. Every turn she takes leads her inexorably back to the square, and finally she sighs and sits down heavily on the steps near her usual spot.

An elderly townswoman—one of the few who still speak to her—gives her a friendly wave and lifts her eyebrows. "You're not drawing for us today?" she asks.

In answer, Keris scowls and pulls a single chalk from her pocket. *Go away*, she scrawls on the ground, in the old tongue. The old woman shrugs and shuffles off, muttering something under her breath about ingratitude.

Keris starts when Arlau touches her shoulder. Arlau's face is very close when she looks around, her green eyes devoid of their usual amusement.

"You know what we have to do," she says.

Keris blinks and says, "What?" But she knows.

***

That night, Keris leaves her belongings with the tavern-keeper, instructing him to keep them behind the bar until she returns for them. He looks as though he is about to refuse, but he takes the coin she gives him. It's her last; but she is not worried, and she doesn't look behind her as she leaves.

She feels her way around the outer wall of the town, the white stone smooth and cool beneath her touch. She fears she won't be able to see well enough to draw, but Arlau takes her hand, threading her dry warm fingers through Keris's cold ones.

"Like this," she breathes against Keris's ear, and together, they draw flames as high as their arms can reach.

The darkness is not a problem for long.

***

Sitting on the hillside above the town, Keris watches the fire. The yells of the townsfolk are muffled, and Keris does not try to understand them. She has Arlau now, crooning to her in the old tongue. She does not need their language.

The trees in the square light up like candelabras, and the sleeping birds scatter, screaming, from their branches. The tavern disgorges a shoving, shouting mass of half-drunk revellers, and Keris notes with satisfaction a few blue-and-white liveries among them. The wisewoman's cottage burns last and longest, her store of incense giving off a cloud of sweet-smelling smoke that reaches Keris and Arlau at their perch on the hillside.

Some small part of Keris hopes that she, at least, got away. The rest of her does not mind; only sits, pressed side-by-side with Arlau, humming the old song, as the town burns. The flames warm her like home.

MEET ME AT STATE SPONSORED MOVIE NIGHT
TIFFANY E. WILSON

Yola's feet drum on the sidewalk. She knows it looks suspicious, but the jitters need to go somewhere as she sits on her stoop. A glance at her phone confirms the FE Patrol is late, but the 27% battery symbol in the corner steals her attention. She turns it off. Six hours into this latest blackout, with no end in sight, it's better to save the battery for later.

There: a black SUV turns at the corner. Painted on the hood is a large white eye encircled by *FREEDOM ENFORCERS* in bold letters. Tinted windows reflect scowling faces on the sidewalk as the car passes. They can't detain you for scowling – not yet, anyway.

Yola turns her head as if to glance down the street, but under the mirror lenses of her aviators, she watches the patrol hum past. When they cruise to the next block, she slings her backpack over her shoulder and hustles in the opposite direction. Thirty minutes until the next patrol.

The summer sun is setting. Tall apartment buildings shade the sidewalk, but the day's heat hasn't broken yet. Sweat glitters on the back of Yola's crew cut and beads down her neck. The back of her tank top is damp.

Fari appears from a doorway as Yola strides by. She wears a faded sundress, her long black hair pulled into a high ponytail, and clutches a tote bag under her arm. Neither speaks as they walk side-by-side.

Every building has windows wide open, begging for the last bits of light and any cool kiss from a breeze.

"I'm worried we're gonna look out of place." Fari keeps her voice low. "No teens go to Movie Night."

"It's the only entertainment in the zone. Besides, FE wants us there, being good citizens. Community participators." Yola realizes Fari doesn't enjoy the sarcasm, and takes her friend's hand. "Just be cool."

Overhead, a man in a stained undershirt cooks chicken on a rusty grill he's wedged onto his fire escape. People linger on the sidewalk nearby, salivating over the scent. Yola makes a brief mental calculation. Since the rolling blackouts began a couple weeks ago, supposedly triggered by a heatwave, refrigerated food delivery to this zone's grocery store has

54

ceased. To get chicken that doesn't make him sick, this man probably used a pass to shop in a zone with electricity.

Fari nudges Yola and hands her a beef jerky stick.

"It's warm from sitting in the sun all day – so it's almost like eating steak if you don't think too hard about it."

As they struggle to tear the thick wrappers, a siren slices the quiet. Behind them, an FE car pulls haphazardly across the road, blocking traffic in both directions. Two men in black uniforms get out, guns drawn.

Pedestrians scatter, faces disappear from windows, even the man with the grill cowers out of sight. Fari spins around, pressing her back against hot bricks. Yola grabs Fari's hand, tugging her to keep moving.

The officers push their way into an apartment building, yelling for everyone to get down.

"Not us!" Yola hisses. The deafening swish of her heartbeat is cut with the crack of a gunshot.

The friends run. At the corner, they take the turn too fast and bump into each other, nearly falling. Once out of sight, Yola slows down, gripping Fari's hand to keep her from darting away.

At the bus stop, they pause to catch their breath. An older woman sits on the bench, clutching a wrinkled shopping bag on her lap.

Yola smiles at her until the woman looks away.

"We're okay. Just made it," Yola says. "Do you want to wait for the bus home or keep walking?"

The woman seems more interested in watching for the bus than their conversation, but they can't be too careful.

Fari presses her hand against her chest. The street is quiet now. No sirens, no shouting.

"I know it's...hot," Yola says. "I understand if you want to go home."

"I'm fine. Let's go."

Seventh Street Park spans half a block: a small open field previously used for kids' soccer and tee-ball and an aging playground. Pete, a middle-aged man with perpetually-red eyes and a bald spot forming on his crown, is setting up the projector screen at the far end of the open field. Once upon a time, he was the music teacher at the adjacent Addams Elementary School, before they boarded it up last year and offered the staff part-time jobs in the new Department of Community Events. Pete is the only one left.

The dimming evening light makes the park even more dreary. Three blankets are spread on the patchy grass and dirt of the field, where parents chat in low voices. Their kids chase and giggle on the creaky playground equipment behind them.

On the sidewalk that divides the park from the playground is a battered metal bench where a young man with black hair sits, his back to the field. As Fari and Yola approach him, they pass a folding table holding the projector itself. Fari attempts to discreetly glance at the ports on the back of the coveted machinery.

"I didn't think you were gonna show." Carlos turns around, resting his arm across the back of the bench. He peers at them over the top of his black-rimmed glasses.

"I didn't think *you* would show." Yola plops her backpack down next to him.

"Keep it down." Fari eyes a man briskly cutting through the park.

"Cálmate." Carlos pushes his glasses up on his nose. "We've got time 'til the next FE buzz by. Fari, you're too tense. You gotta act like you're not doing something that could land you in lock-up for a week."

Yola turns on her phone to check the time. "Let's get set up."

"I've got the corner covered." Carlos hops up and strolls casually across the playground. He leans against a dark lamppost, his face illuminated by his phone as he pretends to message a friend.

Yola and Fari sit down on the bench, hyper aware of every person in the park. They watch as Pete unloads a portable generator from the trunk of his car.

Yola pulls a laptop out of her backpack, its lid covered with faded and peeling stickers: a daisy, an intricate calavera, the silhouette of a rabbit. It's a few years old and a little temperamental. They wait together as it boots up, fingers crossed against a system error.

"What are you doing?"

Fari turns fast.

A mother stands on her blanket, yelling at her son near the edge of the playground. She's not looking at Fari at all.

The desktop blinks onto the screen. Yola jabs the keyboard until the brightness dims so low they can barely see it.

"Last chance to back out," Yola says.

Fari exhales. She pulls a battered flash drive from her tote bag – a late night trade with Carlos for a stack of burned CDs rescued from her aunt's garage. The laptop looks suspicious, but this is the true contraband.

Fari plugs the drive into the laptop.

The video window appears, then skips, the playback jittery.

"Mierda!" Yola hisses, "I thought you tested this."

"I did! It played fine on my computer."

Yola's phone buzzes with an alert. Showtime.

The last of the orange-pink fades from the sky as Pete turns the projector on. Years ago, when Movie Night was a community event, he had introduced a series of vintage Disney cartoons with trivia facts to excite the crowd. Now, however, he has only a tablet of pre-approved programming that FE delivers each week. He takes no pride in presenting it.

The few waiting faces glow as the newsreel starts, but they aren't watching. New warehouse brings jobs and revitalization to Michigan town. Workers in gray uniforms smile unnaturally as FE agents escort them to their first day of work. The President updates his Enemies of the State list after the successful apprehension of eight traitors. Ten new names and photos are displayed on the screen. With the program running, Pete shuffles back toward his car. He slumps down on the curb next to the generator and lights a cigarette.

Yola picks up her phone to check the time. "About five minutes until the next FE patrol. You set up, I'll futz with the video settings."

Fari scrambles to pull a tangled cable from her tote bag. She hands one end to Yola, then climbs over the back of the bench. Casual in her approach, Fari squats behind the projector, hidden in the shadow. Her fingertips trace the shapes on the back of the projector, searching for the right port.

"Hurry up!"

Fari can taste her sweat as she realizes that none of the ports match her cable.

From the darkness behind them, Carlos whistles a short tune. Yola tenses at the signal and slaps her laptop shut. As headlights sweep across the the park, Fari dives under the table. FE Patrol slows to a stop next to Pete. The driver's window lowers, and an officer leans out. While the newsreel credits roll, their conversation is drowned out by a stirring orchestral version of the national anthem. FE drives away as the last notes of the segment fade. In the silence, Carlos whistles an all clear.

"I'm ready," Yola whispers.

"I'm not." Fari crawls out and checks the ports again.

The main cartoon of the week features a group of cheaply animated puppies in gray uniforms. An FE captain tasks them to locate a lost kitten. The puppies trot around their neighborhood, peering in windows to see what people are hiding.

Fari fingers the cable coiling from the FE tablet on the table. She follows it to the projector, bumping against a bulky adapter. Perfect! She yanks the cable out.

The state-sponsored image on the screen halts, then goes black. Parents turn to the projector, squinting at the darkness. Pete stands up suddenly from the curb.

Fari fumbles until her cable clicks into place. A pixelated video bursts into the darkness, its joyful music blasting from the speakers.

Children on the playground stop, turning toward the field.

The image starts out fuzzy, but Fari's chest grows tight as the familiar theme song crescendos. Bizzy strums the guitar while Hector sings along, with animated bluebirds and bees buzzing around them to provide backup vocals. When she was young, Fari had streamed "Bizzy & Hector" for hours until her mâmân took the tablet away and made her go outside. Fari doesn't want to consider how relatively recent those days were.

Some of the children in the park join their parents on blankets, pointing at the screen. None of the parents seem concerned about the change in programming. A few even sing along, words creeping out from forgotten corners of their mind.

Pete advances ponderously toward Fari, following the cable that trails across the ground. "What is this? We're only allowed to show the approved programming."

"Yeah, uh, we thought – " Fari glances back at her friend.

Yola stands up. "It's a treat. Something nice for the kids. It's very short – only fifteen minutes long."

Pete watches the screen for a moment, his eyes glassy.

"One episode," he whispers. "We have to be back to scheduled programming before the next patrol." He pats Fari's shoulder before returning to the generator.

Yola leans against the back of the bench, watching the rapt faces of the children. Fari joins her, pulling more beef jerky sticks from her bag. In the field, families sway to the songs and laugh along with corny jokes. An innocent bliss.

As the end of the episode nears, street lamps suddenly blink on and flood the park with light. Windows glow as cheers echo from the high-rises nearby.

Fari hastily tosses her tote bag over the laptop, but none of the audience is searching for them. They're busy rolling up blankets and calling out to children. With the power back, there are phones to charge, air conditioners to run, and state-sponsored TV shows to watch in the comfort of their apartments.

Bizzy & Hector sing through the closing credits as the lot clears out. There is more scheduled programming to be shown, but the audience is gone. Pete shuts off his generator and begins rolling up the cable.

"We actually pulled it off." Yola stretches her arms toward the sky and laughs.

"Don't get too comfortable," Pete warns as he hands Fari her cable.

"We're going." Yola shoves the laptop into her backpack.

"This was a treat tonight," Pete says. "Thrilling, even. But, it's too risky. You can't do it again."

The young women exchange a glance. Fari shakes her head, but Yola gives her a look: *Maybe?* Fari presses her lips together.

Yola risks it: "There's other...ways."

Pete turns away and picks up the projector, gazing over the empty field. "I wouldn't mind helping with other events."

Carlos whistles, then crosses the playground behind them to head home.

"Next Tuesday there's a meeting," Yola says. "Meet us 8 p.m. at 3rd and MLK. We'll take you."

Pete nods and carries the projector to his car.

Yola and Fari hastily shoulder their bags and dash out the opposite side of the park before the FE car pulls up. They disappear down the street. Cheery guitar chords drift out of an open window above. The sidewalks hum with an energy that vibrates through the soles of their sneakers. Suddenly, Yola grabs Fari's hand, twirling her around. They giggle and dance down this block and the next. As they turn the corner toward home, the music is just a memory as their bodies sway to the beat.

ASK ME ABOUT MY BOOK CLUB
M. MICHELLE BARDON

It is 10 a.m. on a Saturday in June, and the Brunch Babes Book Club has convened at my favorite casual restaurant in New York, Cinder & Salt. We're three-quarters of the way into our current novel, *Going Down*, our mimosas are bottomless, and we're secretly gearing up to commit some felonies against our own government.

I am aware of how dramatic that sounds and believe me, I'd much rather simply enjoy my carbs and coffee and nerd out about literature. But unfortunately that option was taken off the menu when dragons seized control of the government and declared witchcraft punishable by death. Someone has to do something.

Troi stands up on her chair and poises her phone above our meal.

"Tina, the book isn't in the shot, can you move it closer to your mimosa?"

I dutifully nudge my dog-eared copy closer to my glass. Then I take my own phone out and place it carefully askew between the book and our shared plate of beignets, as if I'd tossed it down in a fit of exhaustion from having responded to one too many direct messages.

"That's perfect!" Troi takes probably twenty pictures of our spread and hops back down. She flashes an apologetic smile to our waiter, Patrick, who is just now approaching us bearing a fresh pot of coffee like the saint he is.

"Ladies, I know you're internet famous and all, but if you break one of these chairs the manager is not going to be happy and I *really* don't want to lose my favorite customers! So can you please maybe take less dramatic shots?"

"Not without ruining the composition!" Troi protests, but she mouths an apology as he refills our cups and he laughs it off.

The Brunch Babes are four women: Mae, Helen, Troi, and myself, Tina. We have tens of thousands of followers online who read along with us week after week and most of those followers are, like the four of us, secretly witches. We've spent the past year slowly, painstakingly building up an iron-clad network of resistance. Our mission: to reclaim our country from dragonkind, one book at a time.

Mae leans over Troi's shoulder to watch her deftly select the best picture, apply filters, and run through a series of carefully chosen adjustments to create an ethereal, glamorous version of our table. Some magic has no need for spells.

"Okay. Caption." Troi, Mae, and Helen all look at me expectantly.

"The Brunch Babes are just past the halfway mark, and for once we have a united opinion on the action unfolding," I dictate. Troi types rapidly as I speak. "Check out the second paragraph on page one thirty-one and see if you agree with our assessment that things are about to BLOW! Hashtag Brunch Babes Book Club."

"Hashtag Heating Up," Helen adds.

"You're sure it was page one hundred thirty-one?" Mae frowns. "I thought we had page one hundred twenty five highlighted."

"One twenty-five was a completely different scenario. Remember?" I raise my eyebrows and wait for Mae to walk through the code again.

Three mimosas in the shot means three days from now. "Second paragraph" references our post from this day exactly two months ago, and page one thirty-one means girl, go find your little black book of resistance witchcraft and look up spell number one thirty-one. The phone means *wait for our next post for final details*. The beignets are just delicious.

Our post from two months ago is a breezy reference to how we're all drowning in student loan debt with no way out, but at least we're living that #debtlife together! Spell number one-thirty-one performs data erasure on a massive scale. Put the two together and we're looking to bring a little light to the world by way of erasing every single student loan, no matter how big or how small, with no way for the banks or government to reverse it.

The dragons have multiple chains around us and no easy way out of any of them, but they're mortally terrified of the damage witches can do to their stranglehold. Hoarding is a virtue to dragonkind. Witchcraft, by its nature, is the polar opposite: the distribution of power to any who choose to pick it up. This spell could strengthen the Resistance enough to give us that edge we need to take back the nation once and for all.

"Ah, right, right. Well!" Mae picks up her mimosa and raises it in a toast. "Here's to another week positively impacting readers' lives!"

"To the Brunch Babes Book Club!" we toast in unison.

We spend the rest of our meal loudly discussing the book and as I catch a sleek group of women at a nearby table rolling their eyes at us, I give myself an internal high-five.

In the movies, the rag tag crew of good-hearted rebels out to save the day are always snappy and sexy, with an air of mystery around them and irresistible charisma in spades. In reality, that would get us noticed by the authorities and arrested almost immediately. Our year of quietly undermining a hostile regime has been made possible by sweatpants and ponytails, huge stacks of breakfast foods, and public declarations of love for cheesy romance, happy endings, and women talking about their feelings. Our book club is like a comfy, syrup-scented, anti-fascist invisibility cloak: not only do people not take us seriously, they're almost embarrassed to be near us, lest they catch our unhip cooties.

By the time we have the bill split and our leftovers boxed, Troi's post to the Brunch Babes account has about 38,000 likes. I can't attribute numbers like that to our exquisite taste in restaurants or Troi's photography skills, or even my nigh-Shakespearean talent at writing social media captions.

Times are dark and getting darker and no one has any room inside them to yell about it anymore. It's been less than a year since the so-called election and the subsequent revelations that – oopsie! – we'd somehow let a motherfucking dragon become the leader of the free world and his brood has already lined their roost with the tattered shreds of our Constitution. No wonder all anyone wants to look at are pictures of comfort food and baby goats.

"Have a good one, Patrick!" I say as we make our way out of the restaurant and Patrick waves cheerfully.

"Ave Dracones, ladies!"

I'm proud of myself for not wincing visibly. Ahead of me, Mae catches herself in a stumble.

"Ave Dracones!" I call back. I'll wash my mouth out with a pint of vodka when I get home.

***

Outside the restaurant, Helen lights up a cigarette and takes a long drag, then passes it to Mae. So far as I know, Mae only ever smokes when Helen hands her a cigarette, and I suspect it's because she's too intimidated by Helen to decline. We walk together down the street to the nearest subway station, weaving through an onslaught of bumper sticker slogans, crude t-shirts, and cheerfully ominous shop window signs. *DRAGONS BELIEVE IN **YOU**! PERSONAL ACCOUNTABILITY IS PUBLIC VICTORY!* And the old campaign slogan, still hobbling along on every other car: *DREAM BIG.*

I read a public service announcement on the side of a bus: "Stay vigilant! $30,000 reward! Witches are pack animals! If you suspect one, suspect her friends. Report online or by phone..." I spit on the sidewalk as the bus passes by and Mae shoots me an alarmed look. No sign of dissent goes unnoticed amongst a watchful and terrified public.

Everyone thought things would get better, after the last president resigned amidst the scandal of an illegitimate election. Surely we wouldn't be quite so easy to fool in the next election, right? The damn dragons played everyone. It's still right there in the posters we walk past: WHO KNOWS HOW TO TEND THE PLANET BETTER? THE HUMANS WHO RUINED IT, OR THE DRAGONS WHO HAVE BEEN HERE FOR MILLENIA? DRACONES: TRUST OUR WISDOM. IT JUST MAKES SENSE.

At the station, Troi splits off from the rest of us to head to her shift across town. She stops at the top of the stairs and gives the rest of us a salute with her copy of *Going Down*.

"See you in three days, Brunch Babes. Behave yourselves."

The rest of us disperse – Helen vanishes into a rideshare, Mae walks home to her apartment, and I head to the Magellan Owen Public Library. Who knows how much longer before the dragons realize libraries are a thing, but for now the MO is my sanctuary. My true hearth.

Nobody acknowledges me when I push through the heavy wooden doors and step into the crisp whispers of flipping pages. It's a small, precious wedge of freedom from the watchful eyes of neighbors. I cross the ancient marble and make my way to the 5th floor: periodicals, romance, and a wall of private study rooms.

I place my fingertips on the doorknob to Study Room Nine and mouth an unlocking incantation under my breath, pushing the spell out with only a pencil scratch of sound. The door swings inward into the dark smell of coffee, books, and rosemary hand balm. I allow myself a moment to pause and breathe in that incense of sanctuary as I shut the door behind me, then I take a seat and flip open my laptop.

I pull up a spreadsheet labeled 9 AVOCADO TOAST RECIPES and get to work. Embedded behind the ingredients and instructions is my actual spell, comprised of dozens of cells intricately interlinked with arcane equations. With painstaking thoroughness, I tweak numbers here and there, strengthening the enchantment and increasing its power. I arrange a series of formulas that would be incomprehensible gibberish to most, including my spreadsheet program, until the geometry of magic has clicked into place and I feel the spell thrum at my fingertips. Now I'm primed and ready for the big day. Horizontal lines flicker up my screen for a moment, the magic pressing against my math. I've spent weeks on this spell.

I hit save and close the file just as someone knocks on the door. *What the fuck?* My hands are frozen over my keyboard as I strain to listen for hints of who it could be. No one calls out or tries to break down the door, so I assume it's not the police. I pull out a couple of emergency decoy books and flip on the harsh overhead lights before answering the door just wide enough to peer through.

"Tina, it's me – Mae."

Relaxing into irritation at the unnecessary stress, I step aside and wave her in. "Yes, I can see it's you, Mae. What are you doing here? I thought you had to work."

Mae has only been in the book club a few months. Troi met her at her night job at the call center and thought Mae would be perfect as our fourth – she's forty-three years old and crazy smart; she's a great witch with a real talent for sustained spellwork. But it's like she's looking everywhere for signs of approval to even exist.

"Sorry." And she needlessly apologizes for everything.

"For what?" I ask, opening the door wider and stepping aside to let her in.

"You were probably in the middle of something…"

I finish packing up my things and give her my best reassuring smile. I've been trying to prod her along the path to greater self-confidence, but that path seems to wind along a damn steep hill.

"Nah, I'm done now. And I've always got time for a fellow Book Babe. What's up, Mae?"

"It's just – okay. What if, what if we get, y'know, caught this time?"

Razor-winged butterflies launch up from my belly to my throat and rest heavily on my tongue. It takes me a moment to dissociate from the reality of our situation enough to find my voice.

"There's only ever been one answer to that question, and I know you already know what it is," I say at last, as gently as I can.

The question is heavy with the weight of all the lives that have been lost in the answering. Lawyers don't exist anymore, and neither do prisons. You commit a crime, if you speak out against the regime, hell – if you default on so much as one loan payment, you get put in the dragon chow daily lotto and there's no getting off that list. Unless you're a witch like us, of course, in which case you get burned alive on television for the edutainment of the masses. Rest in peace, Aunt Elena.

"I'm sorry, I just – what if I mess it up?" Mae whispers.

She shakes so much I start to worry she's going to fall to pieces right here in the study room. I put my hands on her shoulders and clammy sweat seeps through her shirt beneath my palms.

"Hey, what's really going on? This is the third spell you've worked with us and our plan is solid. The message has been acknowledged by thousands online. We'll be working this magic with an army of witches. We have more than enough redundancy in the network to make up for one lost working. You weren't half this nervous the first time you worked a spell with the Book Babes. What aren't you telling me right now, Mae?"

She swallows a couple of times and I can see by the way her face goes rigid that she's trying to keep herself together. Something's spooked her good.

"It's Helen," she begins, in a strange, strangled tone like she's forcibly pulling the words out. "She followed me home today after brunch."

Okay and now I'm completely lost. We both saw Helen get into a ride share.

"You're saying she had her driver follow you?"

"It sounds crazy, I know! But I'm certain it was her."

"Alright, what happened after you noticed her?"

Mae speaks in halting, stuttering half-sentences. "I, well I didn't want her knowing where I live, you see. And, and wow. That sounds stupid saying it out loud. I'm the new girl and you three are taking a risk on me and now I'm. I'm tattling on one of you to the other and, and – wait, are you in on it with her? Did you know she followed me?"

Mae's voice rises in pitch by the syllable. If she keeps talking this way, she's going to bring the whole damn library to the fifth floor to find out what's going on.

"Of course we didn't have her tail you," I say. "It's a little late in the game to do extra background checks on you, don't you think? What happened next?"

"I saw someone coming out of the apartment building down the street from mine, so I ducked inside, pretended that's where I lived. I hid out of sight until I was sure she was gone."

"Did she try to follow you inside the building?" Mae shook her head.

This doesn't make any sense. Helen is not only a trustworthy and reliable member of the book club-slash-secret rebel coven, she is also the busiest and most adult-like of the four of us. She has three kids, a real mortgage on an actual house, and a pet sitter in her address book and everything. Yes, she maintains an address book.

"It probably wasn't even her," I say. "You saw some other driver with the same car, I'm sure."

"But–"

"Even if it was her, maybe she just wanted to be sure you got home

RESIST FASCISM

safe! You know Helen's got that mama bear impulse."

I can see in her eyes that Mae's unconvinced, but she doesn't have it in her to argue the point with me. She nods and turns towards the door.

"I'm probably just being paranoid. See you in three days, Tina. Sorry for the interruption."

Mae might indeed be paranoid, but maybe I could stand to be a little more cautious. After Mae leaves, I pull out my phone and take off the plastic cloud-shaped case. I use a fine-point red Sharpie to carefully inscribe an emergency spell on the inside. Then I take a winding route home with a few stops along the way before I settle in with the cheap plastic bottle of vodka mouthwash I had promised myself.

* * *

In the three days since our beignet-filled call to action, my mentions have flooded with *Going Down* discussions from primarily three types of strangers: fellow witches, fellow bookworms, and the malignantly clueless. As much as I genuinely love the book, I'm really looking forward to changing the subject to something a hair more immediately relevant. Like, for instance, secretly discussing the next step in taking down our lizard-brained *Game of Thrones*-flunky overlords.

Troi walks beside me on our way to brunch, adorned in spiky purple hair and red suspender shorts over a faded yellow thrift shop t-shirt that she's hand-lettered the words "ASK ME ABOUT MY BOOK CLUB" on in gritty black ink. I admire the way she manages to wear whatever the hell she wants without getting shit for it by every stranger we pass. I was raised elsewhere on the premise that one's clothes should always be as tasteful and blandly inoffensive as a peanut butter granola bar.

I attempt to imagine exchanging my skinny jeans and oversized sweatshirt for Troi's outfit for five minutes without having a nervous breakdown trying to interpret the casual glances of everyone walking by, and fail miserably.

"Nervous about today's discussion?" Troi asks. I shake my head.

"Not really. This is our seventh, right?"

"Yeah, but it's the biggest… book we've attempted to read."

"Are you? Nervous, I mean?"

Troi shrugs noncommittally and pulls out her phone, evidently done with this line of conversation. She's the youngest in our crew and, even though she's loathe to admit it aloud, I know she sees the dragons eating away at her future even as they devour our present.

"Tina." Troi grips my arm and we stop so suddenly that the people walking behind us mutter obscenities as they dodge a collision. We move to the side and Troi holds her phone's screen up to my face where her Book Babes account profile has been replaced with the words we've been dreading for nearly a year now: THIS ACCOUNT HAS BEEN SUSPENDED.

"Fuck. Fuck fuck fuck fuck fuuuuuccccccc–"

"Yeah."

"Shit! We have to–"

"Yeah, I'm on it."

While Troi tries to reach Mae and Helen, I check my own accounts and breathe a little easier. Mine, at least, have not been suspended. Most of the witches following Book Babes also follow me. We should be able to coordinate the spell through my account instead.

"Okay, they're already at the restaurant," Troi reports, visibly relieved.

"Let's get there fast and hope Patrick's had his coffee today. Did you get a reason for the suspension?"

Troi scrolls through her emails while we walk.

"None. It's just – Oh *fuck*."

This time Troi doesn't stop walking, but picks up her pace instead while she holds her phone screen up where I can see it. Her email account no longer exists. Someone has sold Troi out.

"Did that just happen?" I try to keep the panic from rising in my voice and glance around at the strangers on the sidewalk. Any one of them could be a plainclothes agent of the state, and yes I realize how paranoid that sounds.

"Yep," Troi clips. She taps through several screens on her phone furiously, then powers it off and throws down the next storm drain we pass. "There goes my life, I guess."

"You can't come to brunch now," I say the thought aloud as it occurs to me. Troi shoves her now-empty hands in her front shorts pockets.

"No, I guess not. It's the first place they'll look for me."

They don't know – or at least, shouldn't know, the identities of the rest of book club. Troi was careful that none of our posts ever referred to anyone by name or showed our faces for that very reason. There was still a chance the remaining three of us could pull this off.

"Go to the library. You know how to unlock my wards. I've got a bag of emergency supplies stashed there. Wait for us and we'll meet up as soon as the post goes online. We'll get you out of this." I try to sound like a confident witch in control of her shit. "All of us are getting out of this."

Troi nods but doesn't speak. She's not a hugger and hates to be touched, but damn I wish I could pull her into a bear hug right now. It kills me a little that I can't offer her more. At the next intersection we wave goodbye without a word, then I'm on my own. I check my phone obsessively as I cover the last three city blocks to the restaurant, but my accounts remain thankfully active.

At Cinder & Salt, Mae and Helen are seated at the table with the best light for food photography. *Bless you, Patrick, you beautiful bro.* I slide into a seat and set my book on the table, cover side down – our silent code that something is amiss. Patrick materializes at my side, pouring my usual coffee into a fresh mug.

"Look who's late for book club," he sing-songs playfully. "Good morning, sweetie, anything else to drink for you?"

I shake my head and give him a rueful smile.

"Not today. Back to work after this, unfortunately," I explain. Patrick laughs, hands me a menu, and pats me on the shoulder.

"I'll be back in a mo' to take your orders, ladies."

In spite of knowing exactly what I need to order for the shot, I open the menu and pretend to browse. Mae and Helen scoot closer.

"Ah, Tina, just wondering – where's Troi?" Mae asks casually. "I thought she said she would be here today."

"Yes, it's not like her to miss… Tuesday brunch," Helen says.

"Something's wrong with her phone, so she went to go get it fixed," I say. "But don't worry, she said she's confident we can handle one book club meeting without her. This will have to be a quick one, though. We really all need to get back to work. Soon."

Patrick returns and we go around the table with maddening nonchalance. Banana French toast for Helen, oatmeal power bowl for Mae, and now to me for the all-important code meal for our photograph.

"Avocado toast, please, with a side of bacon."

The signal to action, a call to arms. Green means go.

"Ohhh I'm *so* sorry, Tina!" Patrick pouts apologetically. "We are completely out of avocados today!"

Oh no.

"What? Like out, out?"

"Uh huh, totally out of avocados."

I smile to muffle all of the internal screaming I'm doing.

"You want maybe the crab scramble, or a smoothie bowl?"

I shrug my shoulders, make subtle eye contact with my fellow witches, and incline my head towards the exit. *Fuck it, we need to find a new restaurant now.*

Helen looks extremely skeptical. *You want to just drop in somewhere at nine a.m. in the middle of New York without a reservation and pray they serve us sometime before lunch rush?*

Mae mouths: *Are you out of your mind?*

I nod and grab my book off the table. *Yeah, right now I kind of am.*

"…we have a super yummy maple bacon Belgian waffle on special today, which I *cannot* recommend enough–"

"Sorry, Patrick! We've got to run but we'll definitely be back. Today's just," I flail around for an excuse and come up short. "It's really an avocado day for me."

I throw a ten dollar bill on the table as payment for my untouched coffee and an apology for his lost time and the three of us rush out of the restaurant, into the crush of weekday New Yorkers. We do not stop at the other side of the door, but instead hurry down the sidewalk three abreast.

Mae dutifully scours a tiny map of the neighborhood on her phone looking for a place that's both open for brunch and likely can seat us quickly *and* offers avocado toast. When we picked the dish as our code for "fire up them fucking wands, witches!" it seemed so ubiquitous and easy to obtain, not to mention irresistibly photogenic. Now I wish we'd chosen something more mundane, like pancakes. Or a single triangle of dry toast on an otherwise empty table.

"How could they be out of avocados?" I finally blurt out. "Of all the days!"

Helen stares at me appraisingly.

"More importantly, perhaps, what happened to Troi?"

Mae looks up from her phone. "Yeah, what happened to her? She texted me this morning and everything seemed fine."

I steer them into a small park, just off the street.

"Go check out the Brunch Babes page," I say, watching as they dutifully navigate their phones. Mae's face shifts from confused to horrified, but curiously, Helen flashes a tight, grim smile.

"Something funny, Hel?" I ask. Emergency sirens are blaring somewhere nearby, and I have to raise my voice to be heard.

Helen looks up from her phone and I see it immediately: a greedy gleam in her whiskey-brown eyes, the triumphant tilt of her chin, and something else – a small pistol in the hand not holding her phone, digging in to Mae's side. Mae whimpers, frightened and confused.

"What the fuck, Helen?" I demand. She laughs.

"Honey, you have no idea the sort of benefits package they give a witch who willingly becomes thrall to a dragon. My house is paid off! My kids are set for life! Their kids too, for that matter."

"Traitor!"

"I fucking tried to tell you, Tina!" Mae hisses.

Helen shrugs and clicks her tongue. "Maybe, but I'll still sleep soundly tonight. More than I can say for the rest of my book club besties. Now both of you, let's sit down on this bench over here until the authorities arrive, shall we?"

Mae opens her mouth to object, and Helen gives her a nudge with the gun.

"Sit down, Tina, or I'll have to make a mess of Mae."

I have no doubts as to what needs to be done, but I'm still not prepared for how bad I feel. How angry I am at having to choose between a friend's life right here in front of me and the fate of millions in abstract.

"There's no point in doing this, Helen." I give reasoning with her one last shot. "Troi's account may be down, but she's still out there and she'll see the mission through."

"Oh you mean in your pathetic 'secret room' at the library?" Helen laughs. "The place was raided before you two even left for brunch."

Shitfuckdamnitfuck. I had sent Troi right into a trap. With any luck, the wards held and the authorities walked past room nine none the wiser. But I'm not holding out much hope on that; our luck's been utter trash today.

"Well, if that's the situation," I say, abruptly snatching a large cup of coffee out of the hands of a man obliviously walking past us. I pop off the plastic lid and before Helen has time to react, I throw twenty ounces of what smells like pumpkin spice doom straight at her face.

Before the empty cup even hits the ground, I'm sprinting away as fast as I can manage and behind me I hear both Helen and Mae scream. I force myself not to look back. I hope Mae gets herself together in time to get out of there safely, but I can't worry about her right now. I've got to figure out a way to get the signal out and set our spell off.

Alarmed pedestrians scatter in all directions as I tear out of the park. I bolt into an alleyway, looking up from my phone from time to time to navigate grungy back streets until I emerge across the street from my beloved library. Which is surrounded by police. *Shitfuckdamnitfuck.* I hear Helen's laugh behind me and spin around.

"Did you think I was bluffing, dear?" she says. "You should know by now, I never bluff."

"True," I say, "there was that one month when our book was *Pride & Prejudice*, and you flat out stated that you would never read Jane Austen, even once, because you knew in your gut she was overrated. You could have just lied and saved a bunch of drama."

"I stand by my word: Austen is overrated."

"Why do I never see the red flags people fly until it's too late?"

"Enough. Mae is in handcuffs and Troi is most certainly on her way to the fire pits by now. It's just down to you, Christina."

"Why, Helen?" It's stupid of me to ask, I know, but I need to stall her for just a minute while I finish playing with my phone. "After everything we've worked so hard for, why throw it all away?"

"Because ideals are cute, for grad students and children, but some of us have bills to pay, Tina." Helen never misses a beat. "The four of us? No matter how highly you may judge your skills at witchcraft, are not enough. They will never be enough to defeat what we are up against. And you can rally all the internet dorks you want, but they'll never be enough either."

"You don't know that!"

"Oh, but I do." Helen flashes a self-satisfied smirk. "I know because the Brunch Babes account is locked, you didn't get the photo anyway, and your friends are at the mercy of federal officers. And I hold your life in my hands."

I stop typing on my phone and pause for a fraction of a second as if to consider this. Helen senses my mind at work and continues.

"I don't want your blood on my hands, Tina. Just turn yourself in now and throw yourself at the mercy of our rulers. Maybe they'll be as generous with you as they were with me – in exchange for vital information. Don't you want to be able to buy a home sometime before retirement? Don't you want to be able to afford to retire? Pay off your student loans?"

"No one would have any student loans to pay off at all if you'd just let us work the fucking spell!"

Helen shrugs.

"I have a family to think of, Tina. I can't risk their safety. You should think about your own life sometime, instead of focusing on everyone else's."

In that moment, I realize two things. One: Helen is pointing her gun at me. Two: My photo of a particularly stunning avocado toast from about a year ago has just uploaded to my account with hashtag BreakfastBomb. My spreadsheet spell is set to go off by scheduled macro any second now. We were supposed to be finishing up our celebratory mimosas while it did so, but still: mission accomplished.

"You're right," I say. I hold up my phone as if I'm going to surrender it. I brush my thumb in a particular way across the back and activate the emergency spell I embedded in the case.

Helen slaps the phone out of my hand, too late. I feel the icy-sweet tendrils of magic climbing out from the glyph, spreading around us. Even in my current predicament, I spare a moment of fascination for the magic at work. The spell's a nasty one that I've, fortunately, never had reason to use before. I hope it doesn't hurt too much.

"Whatever you just set off, it's not going to make a damn bit of difference for you," Helen says, though she's clearly sweating about the difference the spell will make for her.

"Maybe not, but at least I'll have–"

Bitch doesn't even let me finish my final quip! Helen's gun goes off point blank into my abdomen and oh, fuck. That hurts. My legs give way, and my own blood pools around my knees, hot rivulets soaking into my jeans, trickling around my phone. Helen's face looms over me.

"Are you happy?" she whispers.

The world spins and then narrows down to my lips; I can taste the herbal-copper sizzle of magic in the air. Our spell worked. Everyone's student debt is gone and with it, one more chain is broken. I hope it's enough to encourage the others to keep going, keep fighting. I hope more witches start more book clubs. I don't have the strength to answer Helen aloud, but yeah. I'm dying happy.

My vision starts to fade. I don't think I'm breathing at all anymore. I watch Helen pick up my phone where it fell and as I feel my emergency spell uncoil and latch on to me, I smile. She's too late. I'm snatched away, along with the enchanted phone and some bits of alley debris, to another safehouse library halfway across the country. I'm conscious just long enough to see the worried faces of friends rushing towards me, and then everything goes gray.

PELECANIMIMUS AND THE BATTLE FOR MOSQUITO RIDGE
IZZY WASSERSTEIN

Dedicated to the Memory of Oliver Law (1900 – 1937), the first Black American to command white troops and leader of the Abraham Lincoln Brigade (Spanish: *Brigada Abraham Lincoln*). Known for his bravery in action while leading his troops at the battle of Mosquito Ridge. – Bordewieck, Crystal, and Lila Camuti, editors. *"We Must Stop Them Here": the Struggle of the Early Antifascists*, Crossed Genres, 2019, p. 3.

***

Is there a connection between the reemergence of dinosaurs and the many-worlds theory? So my colleagues theorize. I can only say this: history is contingent, and much of it is outside our control. All any of us can do is act responsibly. Which brings me to the battle of Mosquito Ridge. – Arendt, Chaya. "The Re-emergence of Dinosaurs: Three Implications." World Dinosaur Symposium, May 1, 1943. Keynote Address.

July 5, 1937

My Dear Eli:
I hope you will excuse my recent silence. We have been engaged in making a barricade against the Fascists, for they seek to take Madrid. We will not let them. I have been slow to write due to a wound, and because I fear that you may not have forgiven me for my foolish parting words. Perhaps I can find a way to say in writing what I could not say in your embrace.
I have been serving under Commander Oliver Law, in the machine-gun regiment. In late winter, I took a bullet in the palm. By the grace of G-d, it did not grow infected, but my left hand is near useless to me now.
I will need to send you home, Law told me. A man who cannot steady

a rifle is of no use to me.

Sir, I will go to Hell before I will abandon this fight, I told him.

Law is as brave a man as I know, the first black among us to be made commander, and a Communist. He no more believes in Hell than I do, but he only smiled and said, well then, we will find a way to make you useful. Pride ran through me like a river, for I have many times seen Law lead the charge into the teeth of the enemy, and there is no officer I more admire.

We plan an advance against the Fascists, to ease their siege on Madrid, and cut them off from their supply lines. I am still nimble and quiet and sharp-eyed, so now I scout ahead.

I can imagine your words in my head, chiding me for not coming home when I could. Even now, I hear you say, we could be mobilizing workers each morning and in each other's arms each night. There are tens of thousands of volunteers, you told me on our last day together, but I have only you.

When I think of the look in your eyes, I feel as though I've been sliced open. But I believed in this cause then, and now I have seen proof with my own eyes: we must stop the Fascists here, or they will spread across Europe. There are German bombers overhead and Italian arms on the other side of the lines. I long for your arms, my Eli, but I fight to make the world safe for us, and I have seen soldiers (of all genders) fight on despite worse injuries. I believe we will triumph, and I will return to you. Should we fail, I take comfort in this, that the struggle is worth all.

I do not know when this letter will reach you. I cannot send it now, for fear of revealing too much to the enemy, and knowing that I have expressed my love for you in a way many of my Comrades would loathe. I will keep this letter to myself and, if G-d wills, find a way to get it to you soon.

Yours Always,
Mordechai

July 6, 1937

My Dearest Eli:
We have made good progress. Our initial attack caught the Fascists off-guard, and they have little answer for the Soviet tanks. While the governments of the world look away, it remains to us volunteers, the Spanish Republicans, and our Soviet allies to push back the rising tide of Fascism. We have captured the town of Brunete, and I scout beyond the edges of our lines.

Our brigade is in position beneath the outcropping they call Mosquito

Ridge. It rises well above the dusty hills and plains. We are positioned to its north, and to the south of it, Franco's forces await us. I went scouting, hoping to assess what defenses await us should we seek to claim the high ground of the ridge.

That was how I found something remarkable. The weather has turned hot, and there is not so much as a cloud to cool us. This is a dry land, with little water. I use the arroyos here to move unseen, and sometimes I find trickles of muddy water to quench my thirst. I was filling my canteen in one of these–the fighting well away from me, and the area fairly quiet– when there was a rustle to my left. I thought myself a dead man. The noises were not approaching troops, however, but some creature moving in the brush. A head poked out at me, something like a chicken's, but larger and much longer. Two wide eyes stared at me from perhaps four feet off the ground, in a face of tan feathers with a gray circle right between its eyes. Through the thick tangle of scrub, I could spy its body. It made a sound like a raven's quork and ducked its head back in the shrubs.

I had never seen anything like it! When I inched forward for a better look, it kawed at me with such ferocity that I swiftly backed off. When it didn't re-appear to further antagonize me, I pulled a handful of bread from my pack and ate my small mid-day meal. I had some hope that clouds might appear before I would have to leave the shade of the arroyo wall. No sooner had I begun to eat than the bird-thing poked its head back out and watched, quorking as it did so. I ate another bite, then tossed a small piece toward it. The creature was clearly hungry, and I had a little I could spare.

It lunged forward and ate quickly, then darted back. It was much longer than I had guessed, several yards long, at least, and its forelimbs were long and feathered. Perhaps I should have been afraid? But for all its impressive size, I could see in its gaze that it did not mean me harm.

With another bit of bread held out to it, the creature edged toward me, wary. Its eyes were dark and clever like a raven's, but when it cautiously took the bread from my hand, I saw hundreds of small, sharp teeth. This time, it did not eat the bread, but carried it between its jaws back into the bushes. The brush must go deeper there than I realized, for from inside I heard much squawking and quorking.

I took one more bite of bread and then tossed the rest into the brush. The eager noises I heard were my reward, and reason enough to go hungry for a few hours.

I did not tell anyone at camp about the creatures. Perhaps I keep them secret out of selfishness–a bad trait in an Anarchist–or perhaps I simply worry that my hungry Comrades would see them as food. For now, I keep this secret safe between us.

I lie awake this night, thinking of them and you. Do you remember when we first met? It could not have made as much an impression on you as it did on me. You were speaking passionately, supporting the Hotel Strike, your voice booming over the crowd. I stood enraptured, unable to look away. I was smitten at once, and hopeless, for I could not then imagine that you, handsome, tall, and possessed of such authority, could love me, reed-thin, small-voiced, and a man besides.

Then you met my eyes, and it was as though a vice, cruel and welcome, tightened in my chest.

July 8, 1937

Dearest Eli,

The heat refuses to relent. It rises from the land in shimmering waves, with not a cloud to break it. It parches this dry land drier. Everyone thirsts. My only comfort is that the enemy must be thirsty as well, and more miserable for it, for our cause is just.

Each day I have scouted and refilled my canteen from the trickle of the arroyo stream. The creatures grow increasingly comfortable with me. They know I will bring them some food, bread, or a few bites of meat. They will eat most anything, but meat seems to delight them best. There are six of them, a pack. Or should I say a flock? They do not fly, having no wings, but they are much like birds.

They like me quite well, these strange creatures. Now when I arrive the brave one I first met, who I have taken to calling Gray Patch, pokes his head out and greets me with a chirk-chirk-chirk that I think means he is pleased. Soon the others join in. They are ragged, and thin. The fighting in the area has grown intense, the heat oppressive, and they hide. They are hungry. Anyone can see there is not enough in this arid land to long sustain beasts of such size.

I cannot help but worry for them. I think of the stray cats you take in and care for as the days turn cold, and so I know that you will not laugh at me, nor at my fear for these strange creatures. I could die at any moment, but these innocents are caught in our war, and each time I am with them I feel the weight of their presence, as though they were drawn to me for a purpose, and I to them.

Does it betray my Anarchism to think such, my beloved? Perhaps it does, but I feel it even so. The world is not as it must be, and certainly it is not as it should be. It is as we make it. Perhaps fate or chance or G-d helps us, if we know how to look. If so, then it may be that they, like you, are

76

here to remind me to be kind as well as righteous.

Or perhaps G-d does not intervene, and it is all only men. If so, men will soon decide much. Little has happened of late, as both sides position and seek out weaknesses in the other. The weather has slowed everything down, but even if the heat does not break, the tension will. The forces are in place, and supplies run low. Battle will be joined soon, and decisively.

This worries me. Fascist patrols have kept me from getting close enough to the ridge to discover their defenses, but I have now scouted the rest of the area thoroughly. They've extended their line to the east, keeping to the hills beneath the ridge. We have moved our line opposite them, with the plains between us. (My friends the bird-creatures are in an arroyo just on our side of the hills, less than a mile from the Fascist line.)

One thing is certain: whoever holds Mosquito Ridge will claim a dominant position on this portion of the battlefield. I am certain we will soon try to claim it.

What will happen to my new friends once the fighting begins? I wish there was more that I could do for them. Perhaps it is my fate to do what little I can. It is not the first stone that builds a bridge; nonetheless, each stone is necessary. May I be a worthy stone.

July 10, 1937

My Dearest Eli,

Commander Law called me to his tent this afternoon. He hunched over a map of the battlefield, the thick canvas blocking out much of the afternoon light. He beckoned me inside and extended his finger to a point on the map. Mosquito Ridge.

Our orders have come down, he said. We attack the ridge tomorrow.

Yes, sir, I said. I do not like the word <u>sir</u>, but Law is a cunning tactician and always leads from the front, and has earned it.

The Fascists patrol the area constantly, I told him. I have not been able to get close enough to judge their defenses.

Law nodded, put a hand on my shoulder. I know you've done your best. But now I need more than that. I need to know what we're facing. Can you get closer?

I felt my jaw tighten. I can, sir, if I leave after dark. We both knew the risk, but I saw this was my chance to repay my commander's trust in me, perhaps my one chance to help our cause.

I'm counting on you, Goldman, he said, and we shared the look of men who might not survive the next day.

I am sorry to write it so plainly, my beloved. I know it will cause you pain to see it put down like that. Even if you cannot forgive me for my words, I must be honest. You were put on this earth to make the world better, block by block, through small kindnesses and organizing the masses. Perhaps I was put here for this moment.

Do you remember what you asked me, the night before I left, as we held one another and let the cool night wash over us?

Tell me, you said, why you must do this?

To stop the Fascists, I told you. I was hurting and preferred your anger to your tears, so I added, you will have no trouble replacing me.

It was a cruelty, and defamation besides, for I trust you completely. To admit it would have made leaving harder, so like a coward I chose the easy path over truth. Never again.

If I die tonight, I pray you will forgive me for leaving you, and for the hurt I caused you. No matter my foolish words, know that there is nothing but death that would long keep me from your side.

Now, at last, I know the other half of my answer. If I could go back and rest with my head on your chest, here is what I would say: I fight to be a man worthy of your love.

July 19, 1937

My Dearest Eli,

I have lived to fight on, but in the strangest of circumstances. That night, I made my approach to the ridge, moving through the scrub-grass and keeping as low and silent as I could. It was long, tense work, full of switchbacks and steep ascents as I moved higher up the ridge. My wounded hand made the climb slower than it should have been. Twice enemy patrols nearly stumbled on me, but fortune was with me and, many hours after I had set out, I learned what I needed to know. There were machine-gun nests halfway up the ridge, entrenched and surely fatal for the attack we had been ordered to make.

My only thought then was to get back to Commander Law, to warn him. I hurried down from the hills as quickly as I dared. When at last I again had a view of the plains between the ridge and our Brigade, I saw a terrible sight. In the pre-dawn light, Franco's forces had rearranged themselves. They had not moved far, merely from one side of a low range of hills to the other, a distance of just over a mile, but in so doing, they had cut off my route back to camp. There was no going through them. I could have gone around, far to the east, but it would have been a detour of several hours. Too late to warn Law.

I made my way as far as I could, through the scrubgrass and the very arroyo I had spent much time in, these last few days. And I despaired.

I sat with my head in my hands, trying to think, feeling I had failed my commander and my cause, when from behind me I heard a familiar quork-quork. The bird-creatures moved in a uneasy pack down the stream, led by Gray Spot. They advanced to perhaps twenty feet away, then hesitated. Gray Spot, always bold, drew nearer, still quorking, tilting his head to one side. My friends were looking very hungry now, the lines of their ribs visible to me even in the half-light.

In my anxiety the day before, I had not touched any of my evening's rations, so now I tore off a bit of bread and tossed it to him. He did not eat, but brought it back to the others, and they devoured it. It would do them little good, I feared. They could not long survive here, not while the battle continued, and on every side for miles there were military lines.

I've heard it said that great desperation breeds great insight. Perhaps it is so. I think it more likely that I seized on the only half-chance that presented itself. It was better than being caught, better by far than doing nothing.

I walked back the way I had come, crouching and dropping crumbs behind me, every few feet at first, then with more and more distance between. My friends moved cautiously afterward, always twenty or thirty feet back. They were clever, and at least as desperate as I was. They were less quiet than I, but we were now behind the enemy line, and no one noticed us.

Halfway up the ridge, I ran out of bread and switched to sausage. Not much longer after that I could hear the Fascists nearby, reading for battle. I feared we would be caught, so close to our goal, but the brush and the steep terrain helped us, as did our approach. They were expecting an attack from the only direction available to the Republican forces, across the plain and up the ridge. I had approached from what they thought was a secure flank.

When I was very close to the nearest machine-gun embankment, I went down on my belly. The skittish creatures stopped, save for Gray Spot, who followed closely behind me. I reached up to him, and he did not flinch away as I rubbed at the soft feathers of his neck. It was my goodbye.

The gunner was already at his post, hunched over his weapon and looking drowsy as the light broke over the desert. Across the plain I saw my Comrades advancing. They were a large force, big enough to not be threatened by the Fascists in the hills to the west. But they had no chance of scaling the steep incline of the ridge under sustained machine-gun fire. In no more than twenty minutes, they would be in range.

Gunfire would give away my position, and my wounded hand made my rifle all but useless, so I slid my knife between my teeth and edged forward. Gray Spot didn't move, but knelt low, watching me with those strange, keen eyes. I had perhaps fifty yards between me and my target, half of that in the open, with no cover. All I could do was move silently and hope.

By the time I was out of cover of the scrub, the morning was fully bright. If he turned around, I would be caught out in the open, the alarm raised and all lost.

I inched forward, quiet as I could. I wished to break into a run and have it all decided at once. But I held my nerve.

Ten yards. Five. At last I was so close I could smell his sweat. I pulled myself to a crouch. He yawned, and turned–

I drew my knife across his throat. His eyes went wide and he clutched at himself as he died, his blood seeping across the rocky ridge.

In truth I did not feel any pity for this boy I had killed, this Fascist, though he was younger than I am. I felt only the weight of chance and obligation that had let me take his life before he could take mine.

I had no plan for what came next, no way to drive my friends forward, but Gray Spot needed no convincing. He came to the body at once, lowered his head and made noise like a pig in the undergrowth. He drank at the blood, then began to feed. It did not take the others long to join him. I could not easily stomach the sight of the creatures' meal, though I did not begrudge them. I moved clear of their way, further up the trail.

My instincts were fortunate, for their noise brought a pair of curious soldiers down from the nearest machine-gun nest, one an officer. They came around a bend and stopped, blinking at what they were seeing. I feared gunfire would send my friends running, so I leaped from the bushes, knife in good hand, and flung myself at them.

My blade caught the officer in the shoulder, and we tumbled to the ground. We rolled over one another, me trying to get a another strike with my blade, him reaching for his own. I was dimly aware of shouting, of the other man reaching for a weapon.

I do not know whether I believe in miracles, but I do not know what else to call what happened next. There were shouts from beyond me, the echo of a machine-gun, and then: kaw-kaw-kaw from behind me. The officer plunged his knife into my side–then screamed as Gray Spot's teeth tore at his neck. His companion gave a kind of choking cry, only to disappear beneath the other bird-things.

It was horrible to see. The two men did not survive long. Perhaps fifteen seconds had passed. There were shouts from along the ridge, and from below. No longer afraid of the noise, I pulled free my pistol and saw, below me, Law leading the charge up the ridge, into the line of fire.

I rushed forward, around the curve in the ridge and toward the next machine-gun nest, firing as soon as the enemy was visible to me. I was dimly aware that my friends followed. Had I given them a taste for blood, or were they responding when a friend was threatened, as any good freedom fighter would do? All I know is that together we rushed into the next nest, and the next, and the next. All along the lines were shocked and panicked Fascists. One crew managed to point their machine-gun at us, but Gray Spot leaped high and came down upon them, all claws and teeth. Fascists fled, pale and screaming, down the ridge towards my Comrades.

At some point, I collapsed to the ground, bleeding from my side wound. I had also re-opened the wound on my hand in the desperate fighting, and blood coated my bandages. As my vision faded, I saw the bird-creatures leaning over me, and I wondered if they would consume me, too.

When I woke, Commander Law was looking down at me. I had been dead to the world for several hours. Long enough, it seemed, for us to secure the ridge and for Law, having seen some of what had happened, to somehow convince my friends to let him and a medic near me.

Those things, he said, whatever they are, are quite protective of you, son.

I smiled. Maybe they just hate Fascists as much as we do, Sir.

Law smiled too.

The battle continues, my beloved, though I am now in Madrid recovering. I will rejoin my comrades as soon as the doctors will allow it. I do not take well to sitting idle, but it has at least allowed me time to finish this letter, and there is a nurse here who understands the circumspection our love demands. She will see this reaches you.

There is much to be done before the war is won. But the news from the front is good, and the day is coming when I will beat my swords to ploughshares, or at any rate trade my gun for a pen.

Yours Always,
Mordechai

Postscript: I have here a letter from Commander Law. It seems my friends will not give him a moment's peace. He says one of the Spanish officers, a geologist, has solved the riddle of them.

You must return soon, Law tells me. These dinosaurs of yours must also be Anarchists, for they are barely controlled, and eager for the blood of Fascists.

MEG'S LAST BOUT OF GENETIC SMUGGLING
SANTIAGO BELLUCO

It started on a lark, really, because I couldn't send Ellie the last book of the Jovian Love Spiders trilogy. Apparently Earth was fine with graphic disembowelment by moon-beetles in book one and explicit sex on the juicy ruins of a breeding sac in book two, but scientists coming up with a clever solution to the Mantis invasion in book three was just too much.

So I did the obvious thing and encoded the book on a patch of skin just below my right knee. Books are easy to compress, so a few thousand cells had more than enough space in their junk DNA. I didn't want to use any of the gene-hacking club assemblers for this, since those are carefully logged to make sure we don't do anything naughty, so I settled for the cruddier equipment in the general bio labs.

I was sweating like a pervert with a potted pig as I stepped into the Houston spaceport custom office, but the military guy there just scanned my hands for traces of contraband DNA with a woefully inadequate spectrophotometer. My teeth were grinding at the excitement.

"Welcome to the Republic of Texas," he said, as if talking to an unusually dull wall. "You must follow the rules sent to you via your local representative." The scanner beeped and he nodded for me to go ahead. Then I saw Ellie waving frantically past the customs declaration line, the thrill of getting my stuff past security bubbling even further at the joy of seeing her again.

Most Martians never got close to the Terran penpals they were paired with in middle school, back when that was briefly a thing, but Ellie and I got super tight. We bonded over bad science fiction and a shared jealousy over each other's lives; she wanted to hear all about the Martian hydro-parks and ski slopes and I wanted all her stories about the epic Texan nightlife. Both of us exaggerated wildly, but that was part of the fun. We were Meg and Allie, pretty much from the beginning.

Of course I wanted to visit her, and after a couple of years of pestering, my parents finally let me, as a spring break present during my first year in high school. Honestly I only think I got it since they wanted to do a romantic cruise in what's left of the Amazon rainforest and this would

82

perfectly get me out of their hair.

Texas that year was just a blast. We went to what I naïvely thought was every club in town and were often waved to the front of the line given my Martian holo-hair that not even the most determined Terran girl could quite replicate. In the packed crowd of twenty and thirty-year olds, we were offered drinks and asked to dance, which Allie and I very selectively accepted, but were always excited to receive. I barely noticed how everything was a bit run down and eerily quiet during the day, and for the first two trips didn't even make note of the rolling blackouts. All I cared about was that the music was loud and people danced like maniacs after getting unreasonably drunk. Not like the dull, carefully monitored activities kids my age were guided to back home I mean, I was a gene-cracking club dork like no other, but sometimes a girl wants to party!

That's likely why it took until well into sophomore year before I thought of sending Ellie books and stuff that were hard to come by on Earth – it just didn't occur to me. Then book three of Jovian Love Spiders was blocked, which just put a sunspot-sized burr on my ass.

As soon as she got my illicit copy, Ellie of course shared it with her classmates, who shared it with *their* classmates, until it seemed like all of Texas had a bootleg file of their very own. Unfortunately, a handful of decompression glitches meant the book could be traced to a single copy originating in the greater Austin area. The first copy was caught just a few days after a shipload of Martian tourists unloaded for that week, but nobody seemed to have made the connection to me. I chalked that one up as a victory.

When I visited again the next year I decided to up my game, this time using some of the shared equipment at the local annex of the Decentralized Mars Technical Institute. I wasn't quite old enough to get access, but since our gene-cracking team placed very highly in the previous semester's synthetic organism design competition, I got a special dispensation. I encoded a whole bunch of manuals on gene editing, several classical novels, and just 'cause I had extra space, Rie Kaz's latest book, a very cool account of the early terraforming teams and their scientific breakthroughs. All real Earth no-no's. I used synthetic chromosomes stuffed into a bunch of my red blood cells, which normally would have no DNA, so the customs office wouldn't think to look there. Not a particularly new trick, but an oldie from the mid-21st century only a gene-hacking nerd would think of.

The moment I stepped out from the Martian territory surrounding the landing zone and into the grimy terminal of the Texan side I knew I was on some sort of shortlist. The bored officer behind the kiosk checking my file suddenly perked right up and walked me to a side office. He used an antique radio to make some hushed calls, then waited awkwardly for half an hour before a couple of soldiers and a woman in a suit walked in.

"Young lady," the woman began, polite in a very outer-Martian way. People from the peripheral colonies are often the ones volunteering for Earth-liaison duties, since they were already used to the difficulties of unfinished dome environments. "Your profile has been tagged by Texan security, and they need to take many DNA samples if you want to enter their country, some which may feel quite intrusive, by our Martian standards. You can of course say no, and I can arrange for your return ticket to be changed for today, in case you want to avoid such unpleasantness."

I just nodded and stifled a smile. I was so adrenaline-pumped that I could hardly breathe. It's one thing to have a panel of bored PhD students evaluate my genetic constructs for design elegance and execution, another to have it tested for *real*.

"Meg, I know you must be nervous," the woman continued, one hand gently on my shoulder. "Just nod if you just want me to take you home."

"No thanks," I muttered. "My friend is waiting for me." Suddenly I really needed to pee.

The woman looked visibly displeased but gave me a curt nod, then sat down next to me. One of the soldiers stepped forward.

"Young miss," he started, sounding rather nervous, "please remove your clothing and place it on the seat next to you, then stand with your hands facing forward." He was quite a bit older than the rest, and to be honest the thick, parallel scars on his face made him look hot in a silver fox kinda way.

He put on a pair of gloves like he'd never done so before in his life and took small scrapings of skin from a dozen spots on my skin, and swabs from inside my mouth, labia, and butthole. Then he uncapped a needle to take blood from my arm, and I began to worry.

"This might sting for a moment."

I tried to look cool as he tightened a tourniquet on my arm, but I was starting to feel the sweat on my forehead. Then I saw the anticoagulant at the bottom of the collection vial and was immediately relieved. They would only look at white blood cells with the sort of test that collection procedure used, not the cells the data was actually in. I felt the need to giggle like a maniac, but managed to stop myself.

I was a bit spooked by this close call, and Ellie looked positively terrified when I was finally allowed to meet her outside. She hugged me tight and made me promise not to try anything like this again. Like an idiot, I thought she was just being dramatic.

But at the time I was totally cool with humoring her. After all, we still had a whole month to party and chase cute boys. At about week three I had pretty much forgotten about the data tumbling around in my blood, occasionally remembering with smug satisfaction how my gene hack passed Terran inspection and the sick cred this would give me back at gene-hacking club.

At one point Ellie and I were at an abandoned factory where there was a rave on one side of the sprawling building and a poetry reading tucked into a side room at the opposite corner. Ellie told me not to go to the poetry area, since it would be crawling with informants, but that only made me want to go even more. I was there for barely ten minutes before I realized it was boring as shit so I ducked out. At the half-broken door I bumped into a greasy-haired kid wearing some black plastic that was outdated even by Earth standards.

"Hey, watch it, you Martian wannabe." I'm sure he wanted to sound annoyed but couldn't carry it through the whole sentence and sounded squeaky by the end. Adorable.

"But I try so very hard," I replied, picking my nose with my middle finger.

He paused, taken aback as he noticed the color-shifting of my hair. "Ah, sorry, didn't realize your deal. My bad."

"Make it up to me with a drink."

Of course his name was something fake and ridiculous, Nobax, and we ended up hooking up a few days later in his dorm room at Austin Technical and Theological. We were barely passed kissing when his bunk bed broke clean in half, revealing a small stash of contraband textbooks under his bedframe – honest to god ink on paper.

"Wait," he shot up, nearly bumping his head on the bed above, unsure of what to do with his hands. "That's not mine, I don't know how all this got here, I swear." I could just die, it was so cute.

"Sure thing, Nicolas." I of course figured out his real name with a simple database crawl within minutes of meeting him – I mean, there are real creeps out there. Plus, this way I could make fun of his awful pseudonym more effectively.

"This must belong to my roommate, or to the guy who had this bed last semester."

"If you're going to be a revolutionary, I sure hope you learn to lie better." Seriously, it was like watching a puppy trying to roar.

After that, I just had to give him my contraband data and swap encrypted com passcodes to keep in touch. My own homebrew of course, the stuff he was using had all sorts of security holes. I wasn't super into encryption and database security, since Ayesha ran that club like it was her own personal fiefdom, but I can still suss out bad ice.

Back on Mars, I was looking forward to seeing what sort of hubbub those gene editing manuals would cause when released into the Terran wild. With it, people could make all sorts of cool mods even with a rudimentary black-market gene assembler. But apparently the Kaz novel was a much bigger deal, and after a couple of months my automated browsing algorithms of Earth cultural images revealed some graffiti on a tumbled down wall in New York of Rie Kaz in profile, just like in her book flap. When I looked more closely, the image seemed to pop up all over the place, in the Republic of New England, Consolidated California, even in the Kingdom of Shanghai. Might have been a coincidence, but I just knew it in my tits that it wasn't.

Next summer, I was pretty busy with my senior year project, and Ellie wasn't too keen to have me back, saying that college was being difficult. However, I really wanted to try out a new trick I came up with so I couldn't help myself. Looking back now, I can't believe how little I understood what I was doing, how I didn't pay attention to what was happening right in front of me.

There seemed to be nothing unusual at the Texan border, but a few moments after I crossed the line two men in a black uniform I hadn't seen before appeared as if out of nowhere. One stopped right in front of me, one just behind, both a little too close.

"You sure you want to do this little girl?" the one in front of me growled. No awkwardness with this one, just a cold, calculating contempt. But I thought I was tougher than that, that I couldn't let some half-literate hick boss me around.

"Let's go, big boy," I said, and the solider nodded to his buddy, who grabbed me by an arm and dragged me off, squeezing tight enough to bruise.

They took me to a much bigger room than last time, one that had a bulky sequencer-assembler crammed onto an oversized table. Nothing like we had on Mars, of course, but it was a good enough one for me to worry.

The Martian rep from last time was leaning against a table nearby, but she seemed more interested in her coffee. When she looked at me at all, she had this dead, flat stare.

The soldiers told me to undress and then took an optical scan from head to toe. Their sequencer was an old model from the 2230s, one of the first machines to use optics to deep-sequence DNA. Before that, people had to extract cells and chew them up with enzymes to get to the DNA, which was very lossy, in addition to being expensive and slow. Optical sequencing, while not able to get as much coverage of the genome as the old chew 'em up chemistry, didn't damage tissue and was much faster and cheaper. The machine didn't look new, and when I looked closely, it still had a sticker from one of the smaller Martian technical cores in the boonies that just got its dome up a few years ago. I wondered if maybe they had better uses for this machine, like at a hospital or something?

They searched once, then had me wait a few hours, then scanned me again. Then again. Nearly twelve hours after landing, they finally admitted to finding nothing.

I'd spread my contraband evenly throughout the cells just beneath the skin, at the dermis layer. It's much easier to infect the outer dead cells, but those are also the cells usually sampled for DNA sequencing. Even if they sampled the dermis, which they actually did at a few points, the data was woven into my genome together with an overwhelming amount of gibberish on the platform of an over-the-counter virus for clearing acne. That sequencer would have to sift through pentabytes of data and even if it got all the contraband bits through astronomical luck, without the key instructions to decrypt it they would still have only random-looking nonsense. Was a bit of a pain to memorize several thousands of number strings to decrypt the data, but that's what all those memory tricks they taught us in grade school were for.

Ultimately, as pissed as they all looked, they had to let me go – strict rules on the treatment of Martian citizens from when we won our independence in the 2160's and when we totally dominated in the Mercantile Treaty War of 2190. That time I brushed up on my Martian rights and diplomatic history, just in case. If only I'd studied the Earth side of that a bit more before messing everything up so badly.

I walked out of that spaceport with the biggest shit-eating grin in history. Ellie wasn't waiting for me, which was reasonable, given how long I was detained, but she didn't leave me any messages, which I thought was weird. But I shrugged it off as just another burst of Terran network unreliability so I went to her dorm room at Texas A&M.

Ellie's room was empty, and none of her roommates knew where she went.

Confused, I went to see her parents in their tiny apartment downtown. The door was open, which was unusual for Earth. Somehow I felt I had to walk in slowly, as if there was an intangible heaviness to the air. There was the sound of heavy scrubbing coming from the kitchen, but otherwise the apartment was eerily silent.

"Anybody home? Its Meg, I'm looking for Allie?"

The scrubbing stopped and Allie's father stepped out for the kitchen. "Did you see her?" he asked, his voice cracked.

"No, that's why I'm looking for her."

His face went slack and he turned back into the kitchen, then the scrubbing picked back up, a bit stronger than before. I stepped further into the room, and suddenly saw Allie's mother sitting on the living room couch, staring blankly at the empty air. I was startled out of my skin, but still not sure why.

"Mrs. Veracruz?" I asked, more to settle down myself than anything else. She snapped up to look at me, taking a second to realize what she was seeing.

"This is all your fault," the blankness drained away from her, replaced by a twisted, pinched rage. "Get out! Get out of my house you alien whore!"

I turned and walked out, not feeling my body move, my mind a blank. The door slammed behind me, the sound so sharp and sudden, like a hammer to the brain. Ellie was gone, disappeared like people on Earth sometimes do – like she often warned me about.

I looked for Ellie all over, not wanting to admit to the obvious. I asked her every friend and remote acquaintance, went to every nightclub and café and bar. Nobody wanted to talk to me, either pretending I didn't exist or very quickly turning away, as if I were toxic waste. Two large men in drab suits followed me the whole time, not making any real effort to stay hidden. I wanted to curl up into a ball and die.

Standing in the line to get into a retro-swing club, feeling like a walking corpse, I managed to eke out a smile to the bouncer. He was a hunking bull of a man full of piercings and vid-coded tattoos. Ellie and I would often flirt with him, half-heartedly trying to get in for free, but mostly for the sheer fun of it.

As soon as he saw me he recoiled, as if punched in the face. "Go away," he said, pointing at me with forced anger hiding real fear. "You're a killer. None of the likes of you here."

I felt so stupid and helpless. Alternating between being afraid that I would also be taken away as well and hoping that I would. After a few days of crashing at Ellie's dorm room a stern university admin asked me to leave, so I went back to her parents' apartment, but they wouldn't let me in. I slept at the lounge area of the Spaceport's Martian territory for three days before I got onto a flight back. I cried most of the way.

At Xi-Wong station, I was collecting my luggage when a woman tapped me on the shoulder. She was wearing the dark blue uniform of the Mars Military Forces, but without any indication of rank, and had a tight bun of grey hair primly tied up behind her head, like a grandma ready to go to war. What a transparent way of advertising that you're a spy. Maybe that was the point.

"Perhaps we may have a talk?" she asked, but it wasn't really a request.

She took me to what was clearly some other person's office and stared at me for several seconds before saying anything. I knew it was an intimidation tactic, but it still worked.

"We would like you to stop smuggling media back to Earth," she finally said. Hairbun Grandma waited for a response, but I was too raw, too beaten down, so I just kept looking at the flawless surface of the desk. It had no cup stains, no minor scratches or dings. It suddenly felt so strange, this idle sheen of luxury and comfort that seemed to be the very definition of Mars.

"You see, Meg," Hairbun Grandma continued, "of all Earth's many nations, those of the former United States are among the most protective of their cultural heritage. You may think that you're helping by spreading technological information and Martian cultural data, but you are not. We can't force them to be more like us, nor is that what they want. It isn't possible, and regardless, we should respect their cultural decisions."

I was ready to give it all up, to slink back to my senior thesis and the petty bullshit that was my life. But at that moment Hairbun Grandma just made me so unbearably mad. On Mars we're taught not to avoid difficulty and failure; to tackle problems with cleverness, patience, and dedication. We are a world of scientists, engineers, and scholars. We build rockets that cut space-time itself and redesign what it is to be human. How hard could it be to confront some petty tyrants lording over their people with outdated tech? Bullshit.

Then I realized that, yes, it was bullshit. Mars didn't want to risk fighting with a competent Earth again, it was in our best interest to keep Earth as a loose collection of perpetually infighting nation-states, locked in mediocrity and ignorance, unable to keep up. I looked down at my hands and kept nodding to Hairbun Grandma until she eventually let me go, looking very pleased with herself. People always think I look sad when I am actually furious.

I blew off my senior project and threw myself to the forefront of gene encryption, on the side looking up every aspect of the equipment that Texas could have, every piece and part sold or donated to Earth – barely any of it any good, of course, charity that never let them fully get things done but that kept them from building substantial industries of their own. We are so very clever.

I sought out people who also wanted to help Earth, but they were all posers who never even went there and had no ideas on how to make real progress. Most groups must have been fronts setup by the MMF to occupy the idly rebellious without letting them do anything constructive. After many months of sending unreplied messages, I finally heard back from Nobax, infinitely relieved that he wasn't disappeared like Ellie.

The next summer came around and I knew it was time for the next trip. It was, of course, beyond stupid to go again. The sane, strategic thing would be to wait several years and perfect my skills, then act when the time was right. But every day I spent in Mars I forgot Ellie a little bit more, found excuses to work less and slide back into my old hobbies and idle interests. My parents desperately wanted to spend time with me, and every time I did, it was heartbreaking, seeing them struggle to keep me close and safe. Soon I would find some excuse to crawl back to my studies, find a stable position as a research scientist or instructor and pretend that I would go back to Earth sometime in the future. It would just be so easy, so understandable. No, it was time to go back.

When I landed in Houston a line of stern-faced men in full black uniform stood at the Texas side, a particularly sour old man in camouflage among them, looking very much like a fossil. They waited, eyeing me, daring me to cross over. When I did the old man's scowl deepened and he made a quick gesture to the side. A pair of men grabbed my arms, put on handcuffs and pushed me forward.

They took me to a massive hangar that looked several years past falling apart. At the center of the rotting hangar was a room with immaculate glass walls, inside of which was the latest state-of-the art sequencer. Even in that situation I couldn't help but stare at the machine with drooling lust. The wait time to use one of those monsters was huge even for senior faculty at a top Martian biotech academy. There must be only a hundred or so of the machines on the entire planet. Next to it stood Hairbun Grandma, doing her best to look appropriately grim. She shook her head slowly at me in disappointment – I grabbed my left tit back at her.

The sequencer was painless, but thorough. Its nanometer-thick needles nestled into my flesh to optically sample my organs, getting fully coverage of everything they could stab at without killing me. Guts, bone, heart, even a non-penetrating scan of my cerebral cortex. They also took copious samples of my hair, gut microflora, the food in my digestive tract, and the microscopic ticks in my eyelashes and naval. My luggage and the clothing I wore was torn to shreds for full-depth chemical analysis and sequencing. They got data analyzed incredibly quickly – it must have been relayed to one of the supercomputers Mars kept in military stations orbiting Earth.

The old army man grew increasingly agitated as the tests went on, occasionally talking to Hairbun Grandma in a tense but respectful tone. She was all reassurance and consolation, and just looking at her made me angry all over again.

They tested me four times and found nothing.

I walked out of the port wearing a baggy dress they hastily found somewhere and a few scraps of Texan currency, payment for my destroyed luggage. Hairbun Grandma was at my side.

"I'm guessing you're here again for some sort of resolution, or maybe a final little inconvenience to us in memory of your friend." Her voice was warmer than before, understanding, even. "This is fine, perhaps even healthy, but unfortunately this is the last time. You won't be allowed back on Earth after this, so make sure to say your goodbyes, and if you aren't on your flight back in a week, I'll drag you back myself. Are we clear?"

I nodded, not really savoring this victory, since my stupidity already cost so much. "Yes. Thank you." I'm sure I sounded contrite and weak, because that's exactly how I felt.

I took a bus to Ellie's grave. I was still being followed, of course, but this would help cement the fiction Hairbun Grandma constructed about why I was back, maybe get them to be a bit less thorough in their job.

I stayed at the graveyard for a few hours, until the early evening became dark, then far past that. At about midnight, I went to a nightclub that used to be a community college, where Ellie and I had gone when we were feeling particularly wild. The packed people were furiously drinking and dancing. I used to think it was so cool how Terrans really cut loose, as opposed to the boring, sleepy Martian scene. Their abandon now looked more like desperation, fighting in some way to forget the violence and misery cutting through their lives.

The men's bathroom had a tiny broken window which remained unfixed for years, much like everything else on Earth. I easily wiggled out of it and into the filthy alley outside. Then I ducked into another cab, then a few blocks away switched to another, then walked for half an hour. I seemed to have lost my tail.

Nobax was waiting at the lobby of a partially demolished high-rise, just as planned. My heart bled when I saw the thick symmetric scars lining his lovely face. They're the telltale signs of torture, a message the Texans leave behind as a warning of what lines not to cross. His brooding moodiness had turned hard and lean since we last met. I kissed him deeply before we moved out.

91

The dingy hair-treatment clinic he scoped out in advance was easy to break into, and luckily their ancient virus assembly platform for basic hair follicle modification was good enough to act as a basic sequencer.

He held my hand tight as I climbed onto the table.

"Are you sure?" he asked. "There's still time to walk away from this." Such a sweetheart, I could tell he really meant it.

I gently pushed him away and pointed at the terminal running my custom code, which was counting down. "I have people standing by," he continued, "we'll get this everywhere, in every possible way. Going all out." His hardness was melting into the cute boy I remembered and he started crying. For just a second I doubted myself. But then I stared hard at his scars and thought of Ellie's empty grave.

The needle will soon pierce my brain and remove the 3-millimeter long tube that is my medulla oblongata, then dissociate the cells and do a deep sequence of the tissue. No encryption, max compression, no wasted space. Billions upon billions of packets of information stuffed into hundreds of millions of cells deep in my brainstem that can only be retrieved by killing me. Neither Mars nor Earth ever considered that a pampered Martian would die for what was right.

My last data dump contains the last hundred years of the Mars Open Library, plus much of Terran scientific and literary culture from before that to boot. It won't bring Earth up to speed, not even close, but it's a start. This is for you, Ellie.

AUTHOR BIOGRAPHIES

RIVQA RAFAEL writes speculative fiction about queer women, Jewish women, cyborg futures, hope in dystopias, and the occasional zombie. In 2016, she won the Ditmar Award for Best New Talent, and in 2018 her short story "Trivalent" (*Ecopunk,* Ticonderoga Publications) was shortlisted for a Ditmar Award. Her short story "Two Somebodies Go Hunting" was published in the multiple award-winning anthology *Defying Doomsday* (Twelfth Planet Press) and was shortlisted for a Norma K. Hemming Award. Recently, she edited a feminist robot anthology *Mother of Invention* (Twelfth Planet Press, 2018, co-edited with Tansy Rayner Roberts). She has been learning Brazilian jiujitsu for three years.

R. K. KALAW is a cranky Filipinx writer who runs on naps, peanut butter, and deadline adrenaline. They will argue that Philippine mangoes are the best mangoes. They have a weakness for craft supplies, a fondness of iridescent insects, and love small, well-preserved animal skulls with full dentition. Depending on context, they either smile or sigh when asked: "So where are you from?" They like and loathe international travel. Their fingerprints resist scanning at inopportune times. They believe family is something you find and build. They've learned home is something you weave together, messily, with strands that defy passports, time zones, and borders. They lurk on Twitter at @rk_kalaw.

BARBARA KRASNOFF was born and bred in Brooklyn, and has the accent to prove it. She has sold over 35 short stories; "Sabbath Wine," which appeared in Clockwork Phoenix 5, was a finalist for the 2016 Nebula Award. Her mosaic novel *The History of Soul 2065* will be published by Mythic Delirium Books in the summer of 2019. When not producing weird fiction, she works as a freelance tech writer; she also investigates what animals and objects are really thinking in her Backstories series on Facebook, Twitter and Instagram (#theirbackstories). You can find her at BrooklynWriter.com or on Twitter as @BarbK.

Besides selling thirty-odd short stories, a dozen poems and a few comics, **MARIE VIBBERT** has been a medieval (SCA) squire, ridden 17% of the roller coasters in the United States and has played O-line and D-line for the Cleveland Fusion women's tackle football team.

J L GEORGE lives in South Wales and writes horror and fantasy fiction. Her work has previously appeared in the anthologies *Impossible Spaces* and *Into the Woods* from Hic Dragones and *The Black Room Manuscripts* from the Sinister Horror Company. She recently participated in the Literature Wales mentoring scheme and is currently completing her first novel. In her other life, she's an academic researching evolutionary theory in the classic weird tale.

TIFFANY E. WILSON is a writer and content creator. In previous lives, she created training programs, sold exotic pets, and listed men's ties on eBay. Tiffany is a graduate of the Clarion Writer's Workshop and her writing can be found in the anthology *If This Goes On*. She lives with her husband and chinchilla in Chicago. Learn more at tiffanyewilson.com or on Twitter @tiffanyewilson.

M. MICHELLE BARDON is a coffeemancer who lives in Oakland with two cats, a dog, a large assortment of plants, and a man she strongly suspects is a wizard. Her writing focuses on exploring social inequalities and resistance to power set within fantastical worlds and situations. You can follow her on Twitter @bardonian or at magicrobotcarnival.com.

IZZY WASSERSTEIN writes poetry and fiction. Her work has recently appeared or is forthcoming from *Clarkesworld*, *Apex*, and *Fireside Magazine*, among others. Her most recent poetry collection is *When Creation Falls* (Meadowlark Books, 2018). She shares a home with the writer Nora E. Derrington and a variety of furry companions. Her motto is "Nazi punks f*ck off."

SANTIAGO BELLUCO lives in Switzerland, where he writes speculative fiction and studies the neural circuits underlying vision. He can be found on twitter @SantiagoBelluco.

Made in the USA
Columbia, SC
10 October 2018